Where Rockets Burn Through

Contemporary Science Fiction Poems from the UK

Edited by Russell Jones

Penned in the Margins

LONDON

PUBLISHED BY PENNED IN THE MARGINS
22 Toynbee Studios, 28 Commercial Street, London E1 6AB, United Kingdom
www.pennedinthemargins.co.uk

Introduction and selection © Russell Jones
Preface © Alasdair Gray
Wormholing into Elsewhere © Steve Sneyd

Copyright of the poems rests with the authors

The right of Russell Jones to be identified as the editor of this work has been asserted
by him in accordance with Section 77 of the Copyright, Designs and Patent Act 1988.

First published 2012

Printed and bound in the UK by the MPG Books Group, Bodmin and King's Lynn

ISBN
978-1-908058-05-8

CONTENTS

I: A HOME IN SPACE

II: HOLD HANDS AMONG THE ATOMS

III: FROM THE VIDEO BOX

IV: THE AGES

PREFACE

by Alasdair Gray

FICTION ENTERTAINS by making parts of the life we know well wonderfully interesting, for describing wonderfully strange lives as if they were possible. Science fiction is in the second category, but differs from other fantasies by taking for granted the scientifically accepted. All fiction plays on our sense of right and wrong. Most science fiction describes the wrong, which is why Kingsley Amis called his book about it *New Maps of Hell*. In 1932 Aldous Huxley's *Brave New World* described a civilisation where people are mass-produced on assembly lines as Henry Ford was making cars. Their embryos are warped to ensure they grow into adults happy with the work they will be given, with no need to choose it. This world is shown through the eyes of a savage who rejects it, and readers will mostly identify with him. George Orwell's *1984* shows how a limited nuclear war has led to sadistic dictatorships with total control of those who are not dictators. What would Orwell think if he knew that a London house has a plaque on the wall saying when he lived there, adjacent to a surveillance camera recording people passing in the street outside? But if you accept my definition of science fiction then two of the world's greatest poems are examples of it.

Dante's *Divine Comedy* is based on a model of the physical universe developed by pagan Greeks and accepted for over sixteen centuries by all educated folk with scientific attitudes, whether pagans, Jews, Christians, Muslims or atheists. (There have always been atheists, though they usually found it safer not to talk about it.) Dante describes the world as a great globe at the centre of the universe, with the moon, sun and five nearest planets revolving around it, this whole system being contained by a revolving sphere of all the stars, which conveyed life to everything within it and movement to everything except the earth. To this structure he added what many today think fictions. Dante's world contains Hell, a huge cone-shaped amphitheatrical pit made by God to hold Satan when He flung him out of Heaven, and all his followers then or since. Dante describes the sphere of stars as both the height of Heaven and of God the first mover of things, while Satan cannot move at all, being buried at the centre of the earth with only his heads (he has three faces) above the lake of ice at the bottom of Hell. After travelling down to that point and entering through a kind of tunnel along Satan's giant side, Dante is surprised to find himself climbing upward – he has passed the world's centre of gravity.

Milton's *Paradise Lost* describes a universe in some ways more primitive than Dante's and in others more modern, because he was an English Protestant who had visited Galileo in Italy, so made room in his poem for the solar system revealed through modern telescopes. Unlike Dante's God and Satan, Milton's both talk and move, especially Satan. On his journey from Hell to the Earthly Paradise he flies first to the sun and, standing there, finds it hard at first to see our world, it appears so distant and tiny.

No poems in this book attempt the epic forms I have mentioned. They are all lyrics — verses short enough to be sung if they were set to music. They show possible (though not always probable) parts of our most recent scientific view of things: a universe of infinite galaxies receding from each other after an inexplicable explosion which generated all of space, time and energy. Our world and our lives are forms of these, and (allow me to say "Thank God", Mr Dawkins) therefore allow us freedom of choice. For two centuries, between the publication of Newton's *Principia Mathematica* and Einstein's relativity hypothesis, the most scientifically convincing model of the universe was made of tiny, indestructible atoms obeying mechanical laws. This meant that the arrangement of atoms composing us in the present was absolutely caused by their arrangement in the past, so nothing we thought could influence the future. Many who would have once have believed in Calvinist predetermination thought it tough-minded realism to accept this mechanical version of it, and regard their own consciousness as an effect, not cause, of what they did, though consciousness was the only effect they knew in the universe that had no consequences. The discovery of sub-atomic particles at first called electrical impulses, and that we can examine nothing closely without altering it, has not restored mankind to the centre of the universe, but makes every mind central as far as it can see.

These poems assert our freedom to imagine excitingly different worlds, however agreeable or hellish. Edwin Morgan's were the first verses to show me that short science fiction poetry is possible. I will not prejudice readers by mentioning my preference for others in this book. I have a soft spot for those which take Lowland Scottish speech into distant futures, but hooray for all of them.

INTRODUCTION
by Russell Jones

THIS BOOK begins with an epigraph by Edwin Morgan. He declared, 'the last refuge of the sublime is in the stars' — and it is from this that I took the title for my own first collection, *The Last Refuge*. It is a small book of science fiction poems, a genre I'd not encountered much at the time I wrote it, other than in Morgan's work, but I was intrigued by the sense of experiment. Science fiction poetry seemed something of a draw to people, particularly events organisers, who often came to describe me as a 'science fiction poet'. Most people hadn't heard of the genre, though over time others emerged from dark space, some having written reams of the stuff, others having 'one or two that might be sci-fi, maybe.' A year after I first spoke to Morgan about his science fiction poetry at his Glasgow nursing home, he died. It was a blow to Scotland, which had lost their treasured national poet, but also to a lot of people who knew and were inspired by him, many of them poets. His death was hard for me too, which felt silly given that I'd only met him once, but perhaps this sadness was because I felt I knew him through his work, that his poetry had informed my own. And so I decided to produce this book, not only *in memoriam* Edwin Morgan but to provide a space for readers and poets to look to the future, to reconsider those final frontiers as he had.

A potential difficulty with a themed anthology like this is distinguishing what *is* or *is not* science fiction. This is a contentious issue, even down to the very words 'science fiction'. Some favour sci-fi, others SF or Speculative Fiction. I chose Science Fiction for its clarity to the wider public, mainly, and instructed the poets to 'write something which speculates about alternatives, with a scientific edge'. My interest was in variety, not just aliens and ray guns (though there are a few in here) but in reassessing the past, speculating about possible futures, current and imagined sciences and technologies, how we engage or might be affected by them. The poets rocketed through, taking their inspiration from books, television, cinema, music, life, the imagination, science and technology, experimenting in form, narration, tone and theme to produce — what I hope you agree is — challenging and rewarding poetry.

As Steve Sneyd points out in his mind-melting essay included in this book, there have been other science fiction anthologies published in the UK. We have a long cultural and literary history in the science fiction genre and this book hopes to bring that up to date by showcasing work by long-established and emerging poetic talents from across the isles. Gwyneth Jones wrote that the science fiction future is an 'extrapolation of the writer's present' and through bringing these voices together I want to create a collage, the impression of which might give us, and future generations, a sense of the implicit concerns of our age and nations. The poems in this book highlight our uncertainty about the future but also a persistent hope that we will be able to see beyond ourselves, to advance as a species through our understanding of each other and the universe(s) surrounding us.

Where Rockets Burn Through is an appropriate title, then, for such a collection: poems for now, poems that burn through our history and into the future.

THANKS

My unfaltering thanks to every poet whose work features in this book, not only for their hard work and wonderful contributions but for their support, good cheer and passion. Particular thanks go to Ken MacLeod and Ron Butlin for their invaluable guidance. Thanks also to Robyn Marsack for advice which helped me to get this book started and finally into print; Alasdair Gray for writing the preface, an engaging insight into the science fictions that precede this collection and encouragement to those who endeavour to explore the genre further; Steve Sneyd for his vibrant introduction to the history and future of the science fiction poetry genre, as well as his expertise throughout this process; my publisher Tom Chivers for his patience, direction and the ability to see the potential of this book.

My eternal gratitude also goes to The Edwin Morgan Trust (SCIO), and his publishers Mariscat and Carcanet, who kindly allowed me to reprint Eddie's poems and to include his book/poem titles as chapter headings. Also, thanks to the staff in the Department of Special Collections in Glasgow University Library. I would particularly like to thank James McGonigal, Hamish Whyte and Michael Schmidt for their generosity and consideration.

A personal thank you goes to Joanna McLaughlin, whose support and good humour helped make the last two years of editing a lot easier. Finally, my thoughts and gratitude turn to Edwin Morgan, without whom the concept of this book would never have struck me. Without you all this book would not have been possible: thank you.

— RJ

WHERE ROCKETS BURN THROUGH

the last refuge of the sublime is in the stars
Edwin Morgan

WORMHOLEING INTO ELSEWHERE

An essay by Steve Sneyd

EDWIN MORGAN once said 'The poet, I think, is entitled to set up his camp on other worlds than this.' Define 'worlds' as not just the What Ifs of our solar and extrasolar planets, but let it embrace other strands of reality, other futures, other selves, and Morgan's words illuminate science fiction poetry's vast array of possibilities. Moreover, the imaginative spectrum offered by the poetry of the trans-real embraces the sciences, with metaphoric wonders on startling frontiers already reached, extrapolating into the even more astonishing not-yet science of future discoveries.

So much science today, particularly at its more speculative edges, provides treasure ships for the poet to loot, whether overtly or implicitly; a poem doesn't have to be bowed under specialist terminology or feature equations to meaningfully reflect on the altering impacts science has wrought on individual, societal and cultural forms and responses.

In the counterintuitive quantum world, the Large Hadron Collider unleashes enigmatic sub-atomic particles, individual and wilful as alchemical essences when Morgan voiced them. How much speculative cosmology offers poets — from the near-mystical puzzles of dark matter and dark energy to the alternative universes? Implicit in String Theory's hypotheses are enfolded further dimensions. What voices might they utter? Or all-swallowing black holes, their white hole 'twins', or postulated wormhole transit to the ultra-unknowable? Or take gene manipulation, already giving trans-species characteristics to existing life forms, ready to create even more extraordinary new ones. Those metamorphoses Ovid chronicled loom towards reality. What's more, with cloning of animals achieved, and of humans (possible if still illegal), next may come the revival of long extinct life forms from recovered DNA.

The evolution of human interaction, with digital reshapings, instant mega-information overload and globalised manipulation of social communication, plus the fast-approaching need to interact with increasingly communicative robot and android labour, demand that science fiction poets respond. How could emotion, comprehension and identity be changed by future designer drugs, or by transformations, perhaps by cyborgisation to part-human part-machine hybrids, involved in the creation of the post-human; how could these challenge the poet's creative empathy.

Such cutting-edge areas of actual or thought experiment offer the genre poet access to the sense of wonder that is still central to science fiction as it was to the very earliest poets considering the world with awe; access to that cosmic fear expressed by Nietzche as staring into the void that stared back at him, which lies at the core of Lovecraft's poetry and prose.

The poet is called on to bring insight to change's totality, summarised by Allen Ginsberg as 'we are all living in science fiction now', whether that poetic shaping be positive or negative, utopian or dystopian, or coolly, detachedly, observational, even metaphorically abstract or fragmentarily experimental.

But why is the poet's voice so necessary? In part because poetry is still an inescapably expressive activity, from all recorded history and far back into oral cultures. As Jacob Bronowski says, 'Poetry is a species — specific to man as science is.' Nor is the activity a passive recorder. As the Science Fiction Foundation's inspirer, George Hay, put it in 1992: 'Technology gives us answers — but what we need is questions, and poetry gives them.'

Science fiction poetry stands on the shoulders of giants, a point illuminated by Sir Arthur C. Clarke's view that to most, 'any sufficiently advanced technology is indistinguishable from magic.' From the earliest surviving literature, like the Sumerian epic poem *Gilgamesh*, poets interpreted a universe whose forces seemed unpredictable and uncontrollable except by magic. To live in such a world, they drew again and again on concepts we today regard as science fictional. To take a handful of instances — artificial beings appear in *The Iliad*, servitors that Hephaestus has made of gold, while the Daedalus myth has him make a mechanical man, Talus, a name revived in Spenser's *The Faerie Queene* for his punishment-administering metal justiciar. In *The House of Fame,* Chaucer deployed what to us are clearly space satellites, as well as matter transmission reminiscent of *Star Trek*. William Blake employs the familiar science fiction concept of time running in reverse in 'The Mental Traveller'. Shelley followed him in deploying this concept, along with equally science fictional moon terraforming in *Prometheus Unbound*. Indeed, that poem draws heavily on the science of its time, including theories of Shelley's scientific mentor, Erasmus (Charles Darwin's grandfather), whose own epic poems of knowledge contain proto-science fiction predictions of black holes and flying machines, later appearing in Tennyson's 'Locksley Hall', raining down poisonous gas from above.

That inheritance from an earlier tradition of poetry was made explicit in a comment by critic Tom Henigan in 1987: 'our new mythology is science fiction and speculative poetry.' As earlier poets used figures of fantasy and myth to explore reality indirectly, the science fiction poet, an outsider seeing more of the game, can reflect on our present, using a What If standpoint in Elsewhere and Futurewhen.

While other contemporary poetry is almost entirely lyric, science fiction poetry does not fear narrative, even sometimes to book-length instances. Genre novels, too, frequently include their authors' or other's poetry, so to illuminate characters or societies, or even to progress the plot. Such embedded poems later served Hawkwind and others as space-rock lyrics.

British science fiction poetry has a tendency to the darkly dystopian. For instance, although the first landmark anthologies of science fiction poetry published in the UK — Edward Lucie-Smith's *Holding Your Eight Hands* and the mass market paperback *Frontier of Going* edited by John Fairfax — appeared in the year the space race culminated in the Moon landing, both almost entirely avoid High Frontierish yea-saying.

That only up to 1969 was a Moon landing poem necessarily science fiction also exemplifies boundary definition dilemmas. Often, deciding whether a particular poem is science fiction, realist, fantasy, horror or other genre, or overlaps, demands context. Is a poem wherein climate change, environmental degradation, or explosive urbanisation, cause our world to resemble inhospitable far planets, science fiction, realist or both? When pollution breeds monsters, is it a horror poem?

Such challenges to tidy boundaries arise again with much of the poetry used by Michael Moorcock as editor of highly influential science fiction magazine *New Worlds* in the 1960s. His choices often frequented the psychological realm dubbed 'inner space'. George MacBeth's classic 'The Silver Needle' used myth-tinged science fiction imagery to convey drug addiction as interior conflict; others versified medical reports of mental illness. There and since, science fiction poetry reflects the contingent relations of inner and outer —'consensus' — reality, P.K. Dick's *idios* and *koinos kosmos*. Using alienation-capable in-head environments such writing needs no other worlds round other stars to find, meet and express the Other's otherness. From within can be conveyed loves, hates, as different as those which will doubtless imbue our android creations, initial portals to reflect on couplings and grievings of future consciousnesses.

Isolation, as Marx-predicted, atomises consumers. Online contact purports to overcome this through virtual community while equally separating us further from 'real' interaction. There is a similar confusion in the paranoia of feeling ever-surveilled, yet choosing to use privacy-busting social media. Also crossover is the painful relief of finding the conspiracists proved right, if not about alien kidnap experiments, then at least about manipulation by a 1% of secret masters. Ones who prove, like an unmasked Wizard of Oz, unable to retain control of unleashed financial forces. An even more frightening possibility to the poet is not the presence of those watchers from here or from Out There, but their absence. Rather than as microbe-like swarms of only statistically interesting experimental subjects, maybe we in our cosmic backwater stare at a god-shaped hole of metaphysical meaninglessness. For the poet, even that challenge, of fearful nothing, can be a gateway to memorable beauty.

The post-colonial echoes traceable in that most anthologised of all science fiction poems, Morgan's 'First Men on Mercury', recur in future-likely persistence of the twin patterns of humanising, for control, the alien Other, and of dehumanising fellow humans into the Other. Science fiction poetry proleptically envisions future conflicts, wars waged perhaps by post-humans: Frankensteined selves, gene-tampered, enhanced, cloned, animal-human merged, maybe with ancestrally-dreamt physical wings growing at last, not for joyous flight but for battlefield duty. Will attack drones controlled from screens thousands of kilometers away, robot warriors, biorefuel from enemy corpses, military zombies and vampires lead us to technofear rather than sexbot technolust? Whatever can slay or be slain in future-possibility, from ancient nightmare reptiles reborn, to uploaded virtuals battling for cyberspace, memories falsely real, can all be fodder for the science fiction poet.

From there follows the science fiction poetry trope of isolated postnukecaust or other apocalypse survivors, stranded in Earth's ruins or as Outer Space refugees, determinedly going on as in Morgan's notable poem 'In Sobieski's Shield'. In such poems the most frequent encounter is not with alien beings met in incomprehension, but with lifeforms discovered through the traces of their civilisation.

This duality in science fiction poetry's relation to its visions of the onrushing Future, near or far, and of the altiverses, alternative worlds perhaps only a nanoparticle-width wall away, is key to its range. To realise the Not-Is, the Not-yet, of those unstoppable Changefields which bind, compel, propel, it feeds on dystopian dubiety as on excited wonder. Wishing for or against such destinations, the science fiction poet must mind-wormhole through from the constantly transient, all but unseizable, pinpoint of Present Now, constantly excreting Past, ingesting Future, like a never sated blindworm, to grasp the poetic essence of its fearsome, hopeful, extraordinary, or perhaps even surprisingly ordinary difference.

A few words on form: science fiction poetry is predominantly free verse but fixed forms do occur, particularly short syllabics such as haiku form. More experimental forms, less frequent, include concrete, cut-up, multiple path, the definitionally slippery prose-poem, and visual-verbal hybrids like collaged and comic strip formats. Ultra compressive, paratactic, and jumpcut material can be found, too, perhaps influenced by L.A.N.G.U.A.G.E. theories or methods proposed to communicate with Artificial Intelligence. Such are likely to grow; likewise computer-written poetry, hypertext, developing multimedia mashups including video and animation crossovers, and doubtless areas as yet unimagined for the science fiction poem. May its future know no limits!

I

A HOME IN SPACE

A Question
Edwin Morgan

They were so anxious, yet they had some spirit.
Some of them shook their fists at us, though mostly
they plodded, scurried, frowned about their business
as we'd been told they would. What was most striking
was that things did hold, the many intersections
did somehow flow through one another, order
without calm did seem to work, not always –
we saw their blood, and bits – but surely something
had ground together in great coherence –
they could not see it, but we did, we could see it –
over a few thousand years of using
their planet, well, badly, up, no matter,
we know and they know there are others waiting
for spade and drill and geodesic dome. Well then,
I cannot relegate, forget, make sense of,
how one of them stood there intently watching –
he was not young, not a fool – a piece of newspaper
caught in traffic, blown then across wastelands,
up among clouds where – and that's all – it vanished?

O

Sarah Westcott

what am I turning quietly and fast
in the great I am, I am here
I am bristling and crusted stripped and pocked
I am teeming and meaning what am I meaning —
where did I come from what cupped me a whole
my core and my aura where rockets burn through
my poles and my gibbons my beautiful girth
I'm rolling round tundra and steppes and snow
I'm playplace and gut, retina, sisal and gold —

space chaplain
James McGonigal

through the northern lights my eye caught beams
of bright and dark like the crown of horny rays
the sun makes from a silvered cloud –
    though luminous these
did not dim the clearness of our target in the Bear
    but rose
radiating slightly out from the earth line

in soft pulses of light
one after another passing upwards
arched in shape but waveringly and with the arch
    broken
that seemed to float   not following the warp
of the sphere as falling stars appear to do
but free   concentrical

    such busy workings of nature
independent of the earth and stretched in a strain
of time not reckoned by days or years but simpler –
as if correcting the preoccupations of the world
by being preoccupied only with   and appealing to
and dated to   the touchdown day of judgment –

a witness to the Zone that fills me with delightful fear

Challenger: A Different View
Jane Yolen

A short time past we worshipped from our farms
Where prayer, like soil, once grimed beneath our nails;
Our skyward eyes looked up for angel's arms,
For seraphim flew not with vapour trails.

The world was smaller then, the sky a bowl
To hold us in the comfort of its round.
We clung to notions of the earth, the soul,
The husbandry of God, the good of ground.

But now huge rockets rise up from that past;
We watch them safe from couches, classrooms, bars.
We see the Farmer, arms spread wide at last,
Sow them like seeds into the shattered stars.

Intae the Ooter

James Robertson

Blacker nor blackest black in deid-mirk glen:
the ship snooves on, nebbin through lourd, lown space,
blin fish in ink. Last blink: wan wee star's face
fizzles and dees. Licht's oot. We're faur, faur ben,
ayont the rax o instruments tae read
or register. Ten thoosan Ks a click
wis when the dials gaed doon, sae did we swick
time's tow? This feels like stasis, no like speed.
Naethin remains but naethin, nae design,
nae truth, nae doot, nae law, nae pynt, nae line,
nae shape, nae sense, nae soond, nae here, nae there,
nae fecht wi God, nae theory needin proof,
nae intellect, nae wecht, nae flair, nae roof.
Intae the ooter noo for evermair.

Our Flight to the Moon
Jane McKie

We polished the silver of our rocket, lovingly,
unwilling not to touch it. We used to strap in
every day, back garden astronauts, happy
just to sit, imagine. After those journeys,
real flight would be a disappointment, stars
less bright, the moon's powder face up close
a plastered aunt, we thought.

But the moon rolled us, glowing in our tummies.
The moon grew, turned its pumice-face around
to scour away doubt. The moon beheld
our feeble blueprints, burned them
to light the way home. Ever after drunk,
we sang *the Moon, the Moon, the Moon* until
we could no longer bear how we had been.

The Man in the Moon
Matthew Francis

i. The Goose Engine

...my only companions a flock of wild geese
that disputed the grass near my hut,
eyeing me when I approached.
They would not be shooed,

but when provoked shrugged into the air,
then folded themselves back down,
the whim of flight passed.

They saw me as one of them,
a flapping biped.

~

The moon rested on the mountain, rock on rock –
you might step from one to the other.
My geese snored, oval cushions
in the goose-white light.

With much time for thought, I brooded on
that icy *noctiluca*:
might one live in it?

Had geese reason? What haven
did they fly off to?

~

Studying their burbling language and coughed cries,
I found no sense there. They would not heed
human words, having no more
than walnuts of brain.

White moved them, and flapping. They would come
to a sheet at my window
for their dole of corn,

fly errands, a full basket
strapped to their strong feet.

~

I rigged the sheet in front, like a spinnaker,
(but it was not the wind it would catch),
and hooked my birds to the struts
in a rigid V.

This shape had such urgency for them
they began striving at once.
The frame bucked, lifted,

so I could scarce hold it down

for the leap of it.

ii. *Flyings*

The lamb, all legs and nerves, was irked by the ground,
kicked it away. Each time it kicked back
with a jolt that arched his spine,
made him kick again.

I tied him to the frame. The geese flapped.
The rag-doll face showed nothing.
A bleat blew away,

and for the space of two fields
he treadled the air.

~

Myself weighing no more than a dozen lambs,
Sancta Maria, twenty-five geese
(all I have) might, at a stretch
ora pro nobis.

The grass raced between my hanging feet,
tilted, and fell. I saw waves
swing past my elbow,

my shadow kicking at them,

in hora mortis.

~

A salad of trees, a peppering of beach,
the great blue flecked with goose-dropping foam,
but most of the world is air
no man can live in.

I tugged at the line to yank the sail
and steer my birds to a rock;
small as a limpet,

it fell behind as the geese
strained for the mountain.

~

Wingbeat by wingbeat we clambered up the sky.
Rock swayed before my eyes. I could read
each crack and blotch of its face,
till we swung over

and my feet dangled on the summit.
We flopped on that cold doorstep
in a field of clouds,

the birds muttering, feathers
still trying to fly.

iii. Lunar Passage

Earth carried on in the gaps between the clouds,
blue and green, fabulous with vapours.
How had I lived there? How long
would I be falling?

The lines tensed. The geese rose above me
like a surge of white weather.
It was their season

to vanish into the sky,
and I went with them.

~

Then we were elsewhere. I felt the earth give up.
We moved too fast for breath, but the lines
had gone slack now, the wings stopped.
We were still flying

in a windless brightness that faded
the stars to milk and water.
Motes sparkled round us:

swarms of cuckoos and swallows
on their lunar flight.

~

Looking back I saw the globe where I was born,
smudged with forests, doodled with coastlines.
That flashing sheet of metal
was the Atlantic.

That pear with a bite out of one side,
must be Africa sliding
east as the world turned,

that oval – America,
just as the maps show.

~

We sailed that lukewarm afternoon that had forgotten
how to get dark, beyond rain or snow,
while the world's engine turned it
twelve times behind us,

and ahead the moon became a place:
the dark patches were country,
furred with trees and grass,

the gold light came from the sun
striking the oceans.

iv. The Moon

There was world here also, a hill where we came down,
a thicket of leaves for us to chew,
tasting of green and perfume,
a view of more hills.

The moon's grip being gentle, one leaps
as readily as a lamb,
springing at a thought

to the height of an earth oak,
landing goose-softly.

~

Trees grew tall as a steeple in that lightness,
and the inhabitants of the place
looked down at me when they came
from heads like rooks' nests.

Each carried two fans of curled feathers
with which to flurry the air
and so leap further.

They bowed low and addressed me,
but knew no Latin.

~

How I was taken before their king and queen,
learned the notes of their singing language,
tasted moon food, smoked the sweet blue
of moon tobacco;

of three gems: a topaz whose yellow
could light up a church, a jet
whose black scorched the hand,

and one of no known colour –
all this you shall read,

~

but after the long night with the cloudy earth
shining its almost-daylight on us,
the rising sun was too close
for me to bear it,

so my birds were shepherded away
and myself led off to rest
in a dark quarter.

I woke from my fortnight's sleep,
the full moon waiting...

space poets
James McGonigal

we wrote poems on charts
by subtle deviations
from the flight-path lines

star gate with five bars
of force which we could climb
to view night meadows

it's quiet out here
so we whistle poetry:
two blackbirds on twigs

star-tangled banners
of space/time shake out their light
like cherry blossom

blank year after year
what kept us alive was this
oxygen of words

to dive in and swim
across to the further bank
with its reeds of light

murky and frigid
those rivers of distances
stunned our hearts speechless

we float like petals
but work like drones in the hive
of Queen Reactor

Out Where Knowledge is Power

Steve Sneyd

"Keepa knocking but
you can't come in" sings what else
can you but old songs
take mind off every old
starhand tells you planetside
happened now really
has dead crewmates follow ship
drifting damaged
through empty black forget why
maths behind it ship attracts
gravity of it
can't go out to catch dispose
port jammed got to thole
how come pleading-looking bump
sightless fish at viewpoint now
and then think instead
something different that world
old inbred Earthmen
stranded sidearm no contact
when arrived all redhead girls
so keen to get laid
pregnant by married crewmen
like him instinct gene
pool needed new strands
even if never rescued would leave

self behind some trace
and forgot name other world
good exchange rate cheap
their kind of science out of
date but still worked had had self
cloned series of him
would grow one after other
through centuries more
like Russian Matrushka
dolls found now all across stars
and if going on
so through future not enough
blot white glare in at him each
think past Omega
Point had heard once takes much more
Energy to get
Rid of information than
obtain in first place
when whole universe cold dark
would be still infoarray
pattern data base
his name essence on endless
spell out Saved I
when this bumping debris gone
forever for good
or in the meantime one more look
find some something block em out
only maybe be
worse know there when couldn't see
them plan to sneak in

Now, Voyager
Jane McKie

Leave the sun behind, its wind
a faint exterior graze,
tattoo of atoms.

Make for open spaces,
shipping a freight of recorded
companions, real ones

by now slipped away.
Don't long for
their particulars;

what used to impel blood
can only tick,
a golden timepiece

susceptible to the shock
of the heliosphere,
the slowing of the solar wind.

Move beyond them into sun-
less time, the subtle
radiant dark.

Alone Against the Night
Andrew J Wilson

I

frosted visor glass
explosive decompression –
I fill the vacuum

II

years without seasons
pass by in eternal night –
lost generation

III
chronic recursion
folding me back on myself –
timeless paradox

IV

our ghosts still haunt us –
things that go bump in the night
things we never said

The Wow! Signal
Sarah Hesketh

      Whatever it was
an alien cough   or the sudden, drunken
elisions of a star   what matters
is that sometimes matter   can be not
that those stern and perfect   canons of the universe
for once forgave the difference
between light   and dark
afforded us   a flawless
           maybe.

Man-of-war
Ian McLachlan

Ploughing a black sea,
full rigged, carbon nano-

tube masts, graphite keel,
white beak and square

gallery, snarl of cables,
silent as a ship in

a bottle, cannon primed,
solar wind bloating its

sails, gunning for Mars.

Lost Worlds
Jane McKie, Andrew C Ferguson & Andrew J Wilson

I. Mars

Through crisp winter air
Mars looks slick with the glaze of two-dimensional fruit
painted on blistered, oil-bitten canvas:

nectarine red,
separate from terrestrial colours,
made more luminous by the buff of being

hung in nothingness.
Children dream of treading lunar surfaces,
kicking white sherbet dirt, particulate and grey when it settles,

scuffing up
the pristine strands of serene seas with their footprints,
their grainy energetic marks.

But a red planet remains a firefly, a promise –
it draws the mind to the scorings, the linear pen-marks
of storytellers

who, for years, have littered its surface
with El Dorados and Erewhons.
A red planet is a rusted arrow's nib

probing beyond the moon, into the dust of us and them.

II. Venus

Clouded by legend, opaque with meaning,
in her carbon dioxide veil,
she steals from the others:
Mars' red iron her lifeblood;
the Moon's wobbling flight round her neighbour
drawing tides for her to rise from, made flesh.

Lightning flashes, with only ash as rain
on a cracked, volcanic surface.
Fault lines radiate star-like;
tectonics-free, pressure builds
beneath the clouds, unmoisturized.

Myth, and reality, kept strangers by those CO^2 veils,
slowing meteorites with their embrace.
She has many names: Morning Star, Ishtar, Light-bearer;
she makes men dream, her earthly sisters
rising from the foam of their story-making.

III. The Moon

Lucian, Cyrano and Munchausen
all told tales of their adventures
on its chalky face,
peopling our satellite with imaginings
like so many after them
until Armstrong's boot stamped on our illusions.

Now the only Man-in-the-Moon
is the face we conjure out of random scars,
someone who never existed;
our minds, subject to phases,
pitted by craters, make up companions.

The God of War stands farther out,
while the Goddess of Love swims closer to the Sun,
opposites with their own attractions,
but our nearest neighbour is the one
who holds the greatest sway,
drawing the tides back and forth,
drawing the silver thread of madness through our minds.

The Moon, this proper noun,
an anagram of a chilly truth:
not home, not home, not home;
but the werewolf in me
hopes it might be
one day.

Hymn til Venus, Luvis Quene

Alan Riach

The message on the screen had read: 'The red jewel
in the ring is cracked. Appropriate, isn't it?'

He stood up and walked to the window, looking out into the black,
and saw the planet there, the horrifying colour of it.

On the desk, on paper, in blue ink he had written:
'Venus, with her diaphanous lace

of sulphuric acid, her green face irradiated
by over a thousand degrees of heat,

is still my planet of love.' He felt the cold
in the empty night. The trembling had begun.

A Barren Moon
Simon Barraclough

It's the one that Huygens hooked
like a duck
from the fairground game
of space.

Entitled *Titan* then,
child of The Golden Age,
terror of men,
closing breast to breast with Zeus;
snuffed out by thunderbolt.

We had conclusive proof:
microbial life
beneath her clouds
and it fell to me
to prep the probe
and keep the instruments
free
of all contaminants
for fear of harming
the alien spores.

Budding
organic
complexity.

Somehow a shred
of humanity
from underneath
my fingernail
splashed down
into her secret sea
and wiped them out.

Our brethren thread.
The second lightning strike
of Life.

Invisible meteorite.

The powers that be
renamed the moon *Remorse*,
after me.

Life on Mars

James Robertson

Aye, Mars is braw, it suits us very weel.
No that ye dinna sometimes hae a wee
bit hanker for the auld country, but ye
canna gang back, ye canna, that's the deal.
Ma son, he's mairrit on a Martian lass.
See, she wis made and bred here, sae it's hame
tae her, and that maks sense. Whit's in a name?
We're aw jist watter, astral stour and gas.
The thing I miss maist? Whit I'd love tae dae
is open up a windae, but I'll hae
tae thole this polydome a guid while mair
afore the ootside atmosphere's complete.
But aw! tae dauner doon Meridian Street
sookin in gusts o ice-cauld Martian air!

Second Coming
Jane Yolen

God is an alien
of the female kind:
birthing sons,
delivering them from evil.
We should know her
by her signs:
the cross of arms,
the open legs.

She:
maid, mother, crone.
Is three.

God is an alien
of the female kind:
forgiving but only
at a cost.
Nothing is lost
that she cannot find.
Nothing is given
that she does not first get.

She:
egg, larva, moth.
Is three.

God is an alien
of the female kind:
do not seek to know her,
to know about her.
She initiates contact,
breaks it off,
then wonders why
you do not call again.

She:
wife, lover, whore.
Is three.

God is an alien
of the female kind.
Stare at her,
you will go blind,
Mess with her,
you will go mad.
Contradict,
you will be gone.

Alien
Sarah Westcott

I arrive at night, touch down
on your counterpane, feet-first,
like Mary Poppins.
All I have with me are the clothes
I was born in, two silver studs
punched into each lobe, a swallow
tattoo, my tongue.

I move among you, feeling
halogen, mistral, gorse-scratch, longing,
my new hair lifting and tangling
under the eiderdown.
The first shit is a revelation,
the insistence of plaque shows me how you live.
I learn to pack my bag with toothpicks,
Pringles, the Lord's Prayer.

Only when I'm swimming
in enormous liquid afternoons
can I escape the circadian,
look beyond the sky.
For years I move beneath strip lighting
an angel hiding in the nettles
and none of you need ever know.

Rave Quails!
Dilys Rose

Swordfish astronauts taste rehydrated space!

Challenge bacteria, dramatic humidity and sand!

Unmanned sample occasion banned!

Insipid spirits lift off spices!

Gourmet hosts greenhouses on Mars!

Moose meat rules for wine and transported spirulina gnocchi!

The major mission of microgravity is gastronomy!

Holidays on LV-426
Andy Jackson

Some end-of-the-pier show, this. *Look down*
on tranquil methane seas the brochure crooned,
take your ease on clifftop walks at fulgent dusk.
Should have checked out TripAdvisor,
Googled up some webcams of the town
before we clicked on *Send*. We're doomed
to an indeterminate fortnight, eating dust
and sandwiches, looking for survivors.

If the winds would drop for just a second
we might hear the scrabbling of xenomorphs
that populate these parts. Tourist Information
recommends the strange Cathedral, worth
an afternoon of anybody's time, and reckoned
to be scene of ritual murder. This far north
the restaurants are sparse, so reservations
are advised; foodies ought to stick to Earth.

We might have roughed it twenty years ago,
overlooked the mutant roaches in the B&B,
where comments in the guestbook set the tone;
I spent a week here and all I got was exposure.
The rain sets in. Inveigled by the arcade's glow,
we change some credits into local currency
and hit the fruit machines, but luck has flown.
The screen says it all. *Game over, man. Game over.*

The Longer the Journey, the Longer the Memory

Steve Sneyd

on this intersystem cruiser
Pluto Orpheus Eurydice messmates
put new crew in place tale on tale
laugh so much anecdotes hard to
follow good old days how put early
Earthies on fooled 'em good and
proper cried in lumps luck of draw
our species faces so like how made
masks of Comedy Tragedy when describe
as laugh is more like gurgle how
you imagine if you sound in vacuum how
populated world goes down black hole
plughole intersperse hiss as of
afterecho of big bang only way to
shut up ramble of old days put onto
what fills corridors as waterfalls
songs of despite what think of Solthrees
never all that overwatching underpinning
shapereshaping to civilise to not
let get Out Here too soon never freed
minds of since retired stint over back
onto between-galaxy stint favourite
song from back there say takes species
as this way beyond their socall minds
to really get most out of got to exist

immortally nearas to understand haunt
line is rough translation goes "The
future only exists because you're
alive" and new crew ownback laugh
behind backs as three leave share –
– chamber as if emotion slid back into
Character she follows he not looking
Back and third he pulling her back old star

Paradise
Ian McLachlan

Buy beryllium off-world,
a thicket of metal shells
in motion, glacial rays
off landing VIP craft,
Buy beryllium off-world,
it's a billion-life hive,
the future building up,
ground level to Paradise,
scraper on scraper,
aliens, half-breeds, people
Buy beryllium off-world,
hopper kids riding side-saddle,
a foot in the air, zip
eastward to Viper Park;
snaked at the lights,
someone shouts.
What speed are we at?

The Event Horizon
Greg Delanty

Perhaps those zones where our souls are said to end up
        are possible: that region the good inhabit,
the zone the imperfect are burnished perfect, the infernal place
        of no hopers. The afterlife is no more unbelievable
than us landed here on this giant spinning-top
        whirling crookedly through space,

especially now the brains proclaim zones
        where time's altered, kaput; dimensions where stars slip
through self-generated cracks in space and so much more
        not dreamed of in our reality. Truly, after all,
the soul may have somewhere to go beyond the only event horizon
        we know of, our point of no return. Unbelievable.

II

HOLD HANDS AMONG THE ATOMS

A Visit
Edwin Morgan

There's another. That's another. And another.
They seem to come to us from their own country
as if they loved us, or found something sustaining
in roofs and woods, airs of blue and pavements,
waters still and wild. Whether they have nothing,
or have become tired of whatever brilliance
it was they swooped from, or are merely knocking
by chance on this world's half-hinged storm-door
because they saw a gleam inside that teased them
or heard some engine-puttering that pleased them,
there's nothing in our universe to tell us.
If you want to help, you must undo your secrets!
If you attack us, we shall not be gentle!
And yet you seem to come and go uncaring,
strangers to solicitation, travelling
who knows what endless circuits that must break here
as briefly to you as we might watch a paper
we cannot read caught on some swirling freeway
before it gusts off white through wastelands into
air and vanished among the cloud-banks.

Celestial Navigation
Kelley Swain

False to say we move toward some undiscovered glory

> Because our blood sings us on this journey
> Because the stars haunt in words only we understand.

Do we think none have gone before us?
Paths mapped to whose satisfaction? Not ours.

> The dazzle and glory of past conjoining,
> False constancies: our sky-pebbles and dust.

This is our chance for navigation, mistakes unmarked until the end.

> No matter how many times they move longitude
> We must sketch our own stories into this skin of sky.

I could learn 'love' in a hundred tongues; speak it from yours.
Can we map each other, or collide, be consumed in an endless
swirling?

> Not toward some undiscovered glory

> Because our blood sings us on
> Because the stars haunt infinitudes

The UFOlogists

Claire Askew

i. Convert

I used to worry about dropping
my keys through a drainage grille,
having my car jacked
by drug-addicts, or developing
some wasting disease. Now

I stand nightly on a wet lawn,
shaking in the dark –
the stars wheeling overhead
like vultures. How long now

before the pattern breaks?
Before they fall out
of formation, and one
swoops down to pick
my bones clean?

ii. Scholar

This is his desk. Steel.
The searing orb of the anglepoise
reflected in the surface like a star.

This is his control tower,
his master panel, Bridge.
Brainwashed: too much science
fiction and *Star Trek* as a boy.

These are his papers.
Plans of spacecraft, top secret,
terrestrial and extra-terrestrial.

These are his artefacts – a track
in concrete, a chip of bone.
It's like voodoo – he doesn't know
how to leave well enough alone.

iii. Captive

He was recording in the cemetery, where it's darkest –
the stars a bright net, and him pale and visible:
a fat, earth-bound fish.

The witness says she saw him implode, fall in
on himself, and when she ran towards his cry,
there was almost nothing.

The grass a little scorched – the smell
of sulphur, and spooled cassette tape
flung over the stones.

We are listening
Sarah Westcott

through the bars
of our blinds at tea-time -
through orange nights
cupped ears tilt
towards the stars.

We hear, sometimes,
the tines of space,
thin and insistent,
constant as light,
as our knowledge of the moon.

There are whispers in
horoscopes
as Mercury regresses;
we hear spring tides -
their reach beyond the shore.

We are listening
in stadia, rising as one,
in choirs and in the sofa department
of out-of-town stores
as light pools onto the Saturday boy.

There are conversations, sometimes,

in Sotheby's back catalogues,
in the grain of very old tables;
a dialogue between barcodes
and desire –

we are listening for an answer
to our selves; why
stars in the vastness sing,
and nothing answers,
answers nothing at all.

Mothership
Claire Askew

I'm sealed like a threat
in the envelope of a well-made
hotel bed, while the nets
hitch up each other's skirts
for passing trucks.
Outside, the pulled-up chug
of traffic lights; a late-night bus's
laboured sackcloth wheeze.

A final spangling bar
of some unpractised karaoke belter.
Blokes. The slam of cabs
and small change spattered
onto paving slabs like hail.
I can hear the banks of daffodils
asleep like clicking light-bulbs,
a lick of river fog along the slates.

Beyond: a freight train's gap-toothed lilt
of boxcars boxcars boxcars in the cut.
The last of winter striking out
with boots and stick to die
under the knowing stars.
A pink dawn spilt like paint
up at the barn. A gritty wind.
The year's first wasp fizzing awake.

And way off, if I pin my breath
into my throat, there's also
you. I'm so far out of range
it's sick and threadbare,
but I pick you up.
The ping of your pale beacon
says you're still alive
under the Spring night's clammy palm.

Beyond the land's dark shoulder,
and the city's thick refrigerator hum.

Disunion
Jane McKie

I took my shadow self to the machine,
fed her to the endless teeth,
her dress a tattered mountain range.

She shuddered at the end,
a captive distance
to the smoky flicker of her frame.

Not equal or precisely opposite,
I loved her like an entangled twin —
dark, delusive, seen, unseen.

The Event

Tom Chivers

On the fifth day we sailed our frozen island out
into the shipping lanes. We counted all the evil things
and cast them in an ice-hole. They were only numbers.

On the fourth day we opened high-yield savings accounts.
The refugee camps were fast becoming commuter towns
encircling the crater. Jets of steam were seen from the tor.

On the third day we left our cars in short stay.
The air was pine-fresh. Pebbles nuzzled at our shoes.
We began to doubt the alignment of the trackway.

On the second day we shopped. You carried your foot
like a dead weight. Some youths got on TV
pretending to be trainee customer service assistants.

On the first day the fridge defrosted itself.
Wearing Halloween masks we made love and
you said something really evil about a mutual friend.

On the day before the first day we fell into geometry
like children. The sky was a chemical peel.
We slept alone and restlessly through the shipping news.

Unbuckling the Hunter's Belt
Kelley Swain

Focus on distant Orion, my fingers rest upon, flicker.

Day is night, crows, wood-pigeons, sing us: bed down,
your fingers in my hair, mouth: sweet riches,

a drunken autumn; an exquisite solstice. Where
are the deepest reaches? Elude discovery:

lead me into your delicious dark soapy-full
salt-warmth and blazing, blazing constellations.

Robot Unicorn Attack

Chrissy Williams

Possibility bursts like a horse
full of light, accelerating
into a star. Explosion. Hit
<X> to make your dreams
crash into stone. Death.
Diatonic chimes of joy.
I want to be with you.
Let dolphins fly in time.
Swim through air, leap
past sense, past sin and then
hit <Z> to chase your dreams
again. *Always. Harmony.* Up,
smash goes the rainbow-trailing
heart again. Again. Again, again!
I want to be with you when
make-believe is possible.
I want to be with you when
robot unicorns never cry, hit
stars collapse in quiet love.
When there is only love.
Harmony. No shame.

Planetfall
Andy Jackson

I suspect it is exposure to the doppler shift
that paints my lover red the way it does.
Once, the subdued winking of the ion drive
would play about her cheeks like rouge,
but now her broken veins connect like strands
of grass, spicules in the starglow of her face.

She might be made of moonrock, a lunar gift
to prove the universe is stranger than we know,
and infinitely more diverse. As long as I'm alive
the X-rays she emits will penetrate me, turning out
my pockets, prising secrets from my hands,
oblivious to skin, and laying bare the visible man.

Her shuttlecraft is landing now; its carefree drift
across the tarmac makes me wonder if she cares
that I am here at all. If anything survives
of what we've been when matter starts to fold in
on itself, it may be this; two grains of sand
in barren space, orbiting each other without end.

Devil at the End of Love

Chrissy Williams

Surprised at the birth of stars,
passions built on noble gases,
the Devil objects. An Angel comes
full of light and carbon compounds
to chase him off with promise,
possibility lit in a single word.
Devil says WIE HEIßT DAS WORT?
and the Angel laughs into infinity.
"Do you not know the only Word?
The Word that wings joyfully
through the universe? The Word
that expiates all guilt, the eternal
Word?" Now is the time for violins,
morsing out in bold metallic bursts
as hands are held, silences broken.
Devil says WIE HEIßT DAS WORT
and there is a solid flash of horizon,
as hearts explode in unending
strokes, a complete understanding
of ourselves. Joy. Flashes of light.
  The singular reality tonight:

```
    \ I I I I I I I /
    –  L I E B E  –
    / I I I I I I I \
```

I Look Up Again

Ryan Van Winkle

It has been so long
since I have seen
even a casual moon

I forget I can eclipse the habits
of my lifetime, dust off my boots
and walk the craters and frozen lakes
of my skull. If anyone asked, I would say

yes to the orbits and satellites, would order a main of impact
basins and finish with freeze-dried ice-cream. I would populate
the dark with ghosts of my own and on certain days, stuck down
here, I remember it all: Summers of burning plastic in the woods,
night-long fasts, the smell of mom's hairdresser; wet, singed hair,

flowered with alcohol and I know there is no honey or blood and no cheese
nor face begging for a flag and how sad I am when myths wane, when I
learned all the chimpanzees, snakes and sounds went up to meet nothing.
If anyone ever asked I would like to say Yes, somewhere out there, yes,
she is a patron of the arts, yes, she pulls, yes if there is anything
but crust and magma I will lift my red nose up in winter and beg
to be pulled like a tide, told to move whenever she is swollen

and zaftig. I might cut my hair in slivers, might darn old socks
and make time to walk outside where I can see but not touch
my lanky breath, might bake a cake iced gibbous and ready
for any ghost who knocks. They tell me tonight the moon
will return fully dressed in her best gambling gown, ready
to be seen as she truly is; as I might one day be known
from a distance in tux and tails. Tonight, I will look up.

Green Lake
Chrissy Williams

Diamond, a fish
tail that twists away
<   > me, bubble
formed in the mouth.
This flood of currents
once a year, a life, lifetime
once a minute, with you
or cut off from you. I wish
I had a diamond
which could stop time.
You know no one can say
how the fish arrived.
These flooded pathways
<   > everything
with light, a blanket,
invisible cloak for the eyes.
This is my lake. Will you
watch fish with me,
brush blades of weeds,
see bubbles swarm, more words
<   > with me.
The diamond is warmed
clear in our hands, familiar.
In this lake the world
ends, over and over.

Haversham Pond

Kelley Swain

For Nancy Perry Kelley, Christmas 2010

She creaks in ossified lace,
porous, marvelling. *Europa*
hides an ocean, Gran — she
will refuse to believe it.

And how could I dream
of that satellite when tethered
to this orbit: skin of bark,
leathered books. Home.

She told me this golden
November morning, last night
she dreamt of swimming:
Haversham Pond. My mother

passed in a boat, threw a rope:
Gran lifted, a swan. This morning
she was happy, her mind treading
recent dreams and past strengths.

There will be no ascension. Cygnus'
neck folds with crippled bones. Dead
stars insist on ancient brightness:
through each lens swims a cataract sky.

Love Song of the Bodysnatcher

Andy Jackson

Come with me, through the stark years.
Together we will ride the glacier,
watch the television with no sound,
take photos with an empty camera,
light cigarettes but not smoke, pour beer
into glasses made from air, hang around.

I'll show you how to find your truest self
in sleep, share contra-indications of love
with you, the pang that's just a side-effect
of chemical imbalances, a rough
copy of a rough copy birthed in stealth.
We adapt and we survive. *You're next.*

Future Dating

Joe Dunthorne

Sat along rotating pine benches,
we wear scrolling badges that display:
Name – Favourite thing – Emotional state.
I am Joe – Money – Anxious
as Porcia – Old buildings – Extraordinary
swivels into view with art deco
cheekbones, sky-rise posture.
She speaks in intricate structures
with witty stucco asides
and is either marriage material
or a one-off demolition-fuck
in a room full of Lego.
I give her green as she dioramas
into Karen – Knitting – Distracted:
her chopsticks clicking
as though making a scarf
from her udon noodles;
our three minutes pass in excruciating
knit one purl one chit chat.
She sucks up her tongue
and draws a frowning emoticon
in the air, before swishing away
as Sylvia – Firearms – Impatient
appears: shotgun eyes, fingers twitching,
a bruise on her right shoulder

the colour of rock dust, she asks
for my favourite assassination,
then lets off rounds
of semi-automatic laughter
while I press red and red
as Kate – Imperfections – Unclear
pulls up with semi-translucent hair.
I compliment her body, her lips,
the infinite detail of her eyes
but she says she can take no credit.
Then she's screaming, quietly,
that her battery's about to die
as she starts to fizz like an unearthed plug.

Phantom Limb
Ryan Van Winkle

I survived and when I awoke reflected
on my hand knowing it was not my hand
though it looked like mine, wore
your ring around my finger — could not burn
it off. It felt nothing like my hand.

My hand rain.
My hand pour.
My hand lifted, held.
My hand folded.
My hand ran.

And the skateboard scars
and yellow tarred tips looked like mine
but when you held it I felt nothing
and let it drape dead. Waiting
for when you would return as you
so my hand could return as mine.

Jan-og-Jan
Malene Engelund

So they gave a twin to his name
for the doubled skull
they had heard ran beneath the skin
of his swollen head.

His missing palate, they said,
made him mute, and some whispered
that he still slept by his mother,
coiled into her like an unborn,

thumb searching his derelict mouth
for what had been lost. That last February
I'm told they found him down by the fields
barefooted in the snow

testing the freshness
of cow dung against his weight,
his body already half gone,
his laugh breaking the orange light

as he felt the crust give in
and sank into the ground below.

The Costume
Aiko Harman

It took three weeks to build: scrap cardboard,
reams of duct tape wrapped around its geometric head.
You fashioned laser eyes out of LEDs you'd found
at the hardware store. I made the arms from the tubes
you'd brought your Blade Runner posters home in.
The legs we cased in rolls of tin foil to match
the leather gloves you'd sprayed with silver paint.

For you, Halloween could not come soon enough.
You promised yourself you wouldn't try it on
until the big day. And come the 31st you'd kept
your promise. Skipped work to prep your robo-self.

I came home to find you in the living room:
a fully mechanical man. You tested
your new tongue: *Beep beep boooooo.*
Not bad, I'd told you, at the time unaware
the true power of your language.
You whirred to yourself in high-pitched tones
while I painted my face.

The party was lacklustre, no costume
could match your handiwork. Unrivalled
we wandered home in the evening, me unpeeling
the sea monster mask from my cheeks.
You, stone silent, your tap shoes clacking the street.

Here, we descend into the uncanny valley.
In our bedroom, I help lift the box from your head,
but find it's wedged skin-tight to your scalp.
You cannot prise the gloves from your hands.
The tubes of your arms fix rigid, flush to your pits
which have turned a grey-silver, sweat stuck, creaking
early onset rust. *Impossible*, I'd said.
You uttered only a long, sombre *beeeeeeep*...
as if you'd been trying to explain all night.

I fight the urge to tear at your cardboard casing
and as we both sit quiet on the edge of the bed
my hand holding tight to your painted glove,
I feel my heart swell full of a cool, metallic love.

The Life Scientist
Kirsten Irving

The mad scientist figure develops from this darkening lineage through stages in which the evil influence is considered hereditary, then external and finally internal to the self.

Peter H. Goodrich, *The Lineage of Mad Scientists*

Mayuri Kurotsuchi hisses: *Nemu,*
bulges veinily through his skull paint,
straightens the greedy lick of his hat.

His pop-out eyes flick over you:
what will *it do next*? He wants
to touch you with probes, with his doll.

His daughter Nemu, whose braid
is a scorpion tail, is not his daughter.
She is his negative, pale and passionless

where he is a king lizard, flashing his frill.
You've lopped off his left arm; blood
and springs, and he's grinning.

Interesting. He stamps the sand
and his earguards – his ears – fly off.
Where they land, they look

like mines, or spies, or ears. Nemu
will collect them later, the flower girl
following the skater.

Also the hat. Also the fly swatter hands
and trashed shanks. She'll tuck each part away,
shaking off the plasma, then disappear

to repair what is left of the body.
What is left of Kurotsuchi?
Always blood in the bank of Nemu,

a daughter he can sever and sever, oh,
a daughter to drain with steel and tubes
taking clippings, the odd swatch of skin

to rebuild, renew, improve his muscles
and maddening detachments. That grid
of teeth. Hang on to the head

that chatters from beneath your heel,
that requests your body, describes your body,
lists what it wants from your body. Hang on

to the head or it will roll all the way back
to the lab, the rack of replacement limbs,
the next experiment.

Red Ribbon
Ian McLachlan

After the pain killers have kicked in
I set to with a surgical knife, serviettes
and a little je ne sais quoi. I picked up
a following, they asked me to do a live show,
offered big bucks. No. Privacy's part of it.
Give me a bathroom in a state hotel with
white tiles, a high watt bulb, some quality
hand soap. This is my studio.

Camera light's on red. I'm half done.
Clean lines, sponge for splash. Critics
call it a gore-fest; it's art. Twenty-three
billion hits. Can't argue with that. I've had
copycats, but the public still comes to
Red Ribbon for an authentic job. There.
Like a foreign object's leisurely advent,
parting lips, flush white teeth, a smile.

Savant, Ward 3B

Kona Macphee

I hear the plaint of metals strummed
by alternating current. Hums;
transformers. Wires like veins,
like skeins of cello strings.
Extend your fingers. Longer. Feel
the nervy thrum that builds below
your middle knuckles. Yes. You see?
They say blood sings.

Time? Continuum. It spans
from over by the door to here
above the bedhead, pinned
by habit to the wall.
At night, the silvered minutes inch
along it. Raindrops; washing-line.
Tell me, am I the only one
who sees them fall?

Check-up
Kirsten Irving

My pulse is not so much normal as superb,
and Dr Bryson asks me to extend my legs, then
hold them above the table, clamped together in a barb,

remarking, yup, you could see those crushing a man.
It's a joke. I'm not the kind and he's at my throat,
murmuring, *good shape, good definition.*

The olfactory check requires a flashlight
and I tilt my head, letting the bulb probe the glued
flaps of my nose, as the doctor pencils a note.

I tell him bright lights, even now, undo
all of the inhibitors in me. My mind gropes
so quickly for the inquisition chair I was slung into.

You should be pleased, he says. *All of us hope
our memories will last. Your kind can at least
select and cut.* I tell him, no, though the rope

and the pincers crouch in my sleep like beasts,
I do not want to lose them, do not want
to forget and return, once again greased

for the mission. I tell him about the marble font
at the cathedral, about the nettles springing
up through the park, gravel, crushed paper, mint,

and say before they placed a hot metal ring
on my eyes, before they sent my remains
back to you as scrap, I never noticed such things.

Bryson motions me to dress. He explains
my new regimen and I agree to everything.
My respray is dry. It looks like rain.

The Last Human
Kona Macphee

She was our glorious mistake, a child that grew
as buildings grow: straight up, then not at all;
dynamics reaching stasis; a waterfall that froze
and glittered in the sun; a perfect blossom
sealed in the acrylic of a paper-weight.

When were we sure? One decade on, or two?
Her changeless features made the timescale moot.
That ever-nineteen gaze surveyed our world
from newscasts, posters, magazines,
and all too soon from mirrors: her cool trick,
the knack that filliped age and death,
we failed to borrow – so we filched her soul.

Conquering the world in a billion faultless copies,
her carbon-backboned DNA became a virus,
a loved disease (for who could look
their own child in the eye, and tell her that
alone among her classmates she would age,
would die, and by a willed abstention?);
and then that first one's quirk – incurable sterility –
became the price our pea-pod daughters paid
for immortality, the keyless lock
that sealed the door behind them.

Now, at last, I have become the talking point,
the outlier that once she was: a long-lived freak
of nature, not laboratory. The lines,
the stories of my skin are newsprint in an age
that needs no paper: all that dies
a natural death, dies one last time today;

and now, the golden sisters gather round
my bed, its antique curio of flesh:
one strokes my hair, one holds my hand,
and as I go, I look into their face.

Second Life
Ian McLachlan

Back when we were billionaire playboys
they showed me my body, naked, newly grown,
a perfect specimen floating in its tank
like a prize vegetable, like a Gucci suit,
beautifully cut, a dandy's daydream.

I was already seeing myself in Las Vegas
with blondes I'd not paid to be there,
tossing down my hand, Ace, King, Queen,
Jack, Ten of Hearts, we were all laughing,
when they wheeled me through the green door.

Sunday, bloody Sunday, lugging a case of
sweetly steaming shirts from Al's launderette,
lithe and bonny, I haven't felt a thing since,
under rain-filled clouds mouthing the 108 names
of Vishnu, and then the 108 names of Balaji.

Apotheosis
Barnaby Tidman

Newspapers pile to cyan few,
used garden gives way/ to deep-hid highwhite
memory strewn; before the dawn came
streaking roll-throughs/ he'd lived through years
of unnamed days, fat with light
of melting lands, with their yellow time,
infinite sands.

Dressing himself, it was like he'd twisted his soul
in the flesh; looking back
returned his face.

The gas stove crowned cones. Objects reversed
from his fingers. A dull white sea above the station,
the cafe,

the school children. It struck him, 'Why wear shirts?' The month
unknown, sky per usual
hidden, fat wasp crawling,

melted varnish. 'Dressing for the morning.' Acquaintances came,
bawled 'What you saying?' 'Hey, what you saying?'
aggressive boredom,

he dragged a cigarette through himself. But there ('Why wear
                                        buttons?')
up the pub window, specks filtering: light wiped up, grime
                                        catalysing
other sunlight,

made of moment: the lorry's sound, smearing the outside/
his living room green, hosting stub-light.
Music both spontaneous

and formulaic/ pummelled ideas harmonious, took him aloft
and dropped in neon-- but reading in the chair, after an hour,
the world mutated:

objects were written. Nervously, ashing tea cups/ friends lost
in forest of text/ the world was impenetrable; mediated;
he left the house

lit by traffic-light, the world a distant strata of noumena.
He navigated blind-sides
layered with greystone; he was out in marshlands, peeling the
                                        world away;

on mouldy alleys
raised to the coastline
the winds stripped script, spun his mind around.
Through grainy floodlines, grey spires
a rare and arch notation
he finds himself in eastern city, Saxon tide lines: as the morning
                                        rubs

flesh from the sky,
the hedges' curled wires
forecast suburban automaton,
Over the furrows it flies,
paid with two final coins for the guardian/
with youth in carriage feigning sleep/ yawns/ standing,
as if in a routine, he produces butter knife/
says 'What *yous* laffin at?
There's nowt wrong wi' me knife —
I'll bread and butter yer with it!' Memory protector, defecting from
                                               age
regurgitates stations,
approaches slicing towns with thin hung wire
the night-raid killed amnesia. The story emerged
from its home of the past: distant in sleep, his father
had taken him, through the kitchen, out to salt flats:
upside-hanged tree trunks, lobotomy, sacrifice, blunted

knifing. He'd escaped: was discovered by reservoir,
the tanks for an Edwardian clerks' dormitory suburb —
and how close it comes, how taunting, to missing the root;
to seeing madness as objective. And as Artemis he spreads
the East to the East, the ceremony completed with laughter,
the flames of concrete rolling in swathes
of a newly minted metropolis. The marshy pits rolled down and
                                               sank,
and hatching out the minarets of a new Byzantium,
strange algae bit into the rocks all around.

III

FROM THE VIDEO BOX

A Dream of Fair Waters
Edwin Morgan

In retrospect, it might have been a throbbing
more than a pounding, but we smelt salt, seaweed,
all those shrimpy crunchy tideline markers,
what could there be beyond the dunes but ocean?
Over the last rise, and down we came upon it,
stumbling through soft sand towards the glitter
of blue and silver that broke over a slither
of stranded kelp-fronds; jumping, calling, whooping
we made it, shoes off, dying for the splashing
that would refrisk us from a week of trekking.
How we swore then, wading light, not water!
It seemed a fearful swick to us so sweaty,
and many said so, though some sat and wondered
how it was done, admiring from all angles
waves that came in only just too even,
with such a finely synthesised deep crashing
it was only just too low to be the sea's. We
had to think it might be radiation,
feet falling off, madness, enemies grinning
beyond the horizon. I said that was nonsense.
– Yes, but you don't have any explanation!
– Why do you think I need one?
                              On a signal
I led the doubters out into that dazzle.
Our leggings and shirts crackled faintly, painless.

The shore shelved until our heads bobbed blueness –
should we go on? We were dry. It was like living
in a rainbow. It was like living in a catfish.
We were all rather high. As I strained forward
with eyes fixed on a dark shape in the distance
I shouted Back, go back! The light's not holding!
And everyone could see the long black tanker.
Its deadweight churned through what was not not water.

We struggled to the beach and shook our sparks off.
One more lost chance to bag the interfaces!

In Mobius
Aiko Harman

The three chasing arrows pinned man to the planet.
Collection, process, use. Each manufactured good
became a tear in the fabric of mankind.
Countries fought to choose who'd bear the cost
of all recycling. The market remained volatile.
The war had milked the land of raw resources.

Efforts flagged. The Ragmen scavenged the last bits
of parchment, metal, terrafibre, cut rubber, ore-fire.
The last classic Chevy Syntex was scrapped in '39.
No heirloom silverware or cherished love letter
tucked up in a cupboard could be spared.
A crime against country, those few
who found 'holding' refused to share
their stash of family photos, kept wrapping paper,
or relics of styrofoam food packaging.

By the '40s, there was nothing. Those who cared
for the planet, bore the brunt of the post-war front:
growing environmental concern and an ever-increasing
post-Boom generation of elderly left most hopeless.
*How would we feed the people if we could not fuel
the Machines?* They conserved energy. Studied
biodegradables. Searched for unthinkable fuels.
Could *Man* be a resource? The strong went dormant,

hid underground, but stalked at dusk, scavenging
the fallen. The kerbside collections began:
the young left their dead at first darkness to be taken
for the good of mankind, *the good of the nation*.

The number of recycling programmes increased.
Approximately 8 thousand routes ran in '51.
Twenty million tonnes composted, fed by truck-full
into the gullet of the Machines.

The Diplomats preached the Old Words from memory:
Recycling reduces the raw materials required.
Maintain core levels to minimise risk to humans.
The ultimate benefits are clear:
clean air, water and better health for all.

Soon the missing persons lists became untenable.
The online cache overflowed with poster atop poster
pleading, 'Have you seen this man?', 'Where is my mother?'
Notices of 'How much for an 86-year-old? Uplift included.'
were quickly taken down but not unnoticed.

The population purge near completion, and 'stock' depleted,
the Machines ground to a halt. The planet bereft
of all resources, no tumbleweed or stray sheet of paper left
to flutter across the empty city streets, silence
became a vacuum.

Few of Those Who Remain remember the old world.
They seldom speak, live alone, forage what they can,
and build nothing.

Torn Page from a Chapter on Ray Guns
Jon Stone

AM Low's 1937 Adrift in the Stratosphere, attacked by radium rays from
Mars develop symptoms which force them outdoors. Luckily, their ship's
instruction manual describes how to switch on the anti-radium ray. EE
operas are full of garish and irresistible rays bouncing off force scree
grandiose ray-gun is the sunbeam (this was the era of vacuum-tube
the entire output of the Sun on an invasion force.
WE Johns of Biggles fame gave us Death Rays of Ardilla (195
weapons are a conveniently slow-moving form of radiation which
flooring your ship's accelerator. In Arthur C Clarke's Earthlight
weapon becomes a stream of white-hot molten iron that punches
spaceships. In Colin Kapp's Transfinite Man, 'sodium lamps
penetrate your skin and catch fire. Sunblock is no help.
In Robert A. Heinlein's Sixth Column the horrible 'Pan
USA, which fights back with ray technology that can tune
invaders instantly, their proteins coagulating like a boiled
stun guns have been a standard science fiction prop since
fall over unconvincingly") was a latecomer. Other
nervous system, like Asimov's neuronic whip,
"Berserker" killing machines, implacable
But the death ray in Silence is Dead
new electro-gravitic and magneto —
In Stephen Baxter's Xee
starbreaker is a modest hand
destabilise stars. Its red out
gravity waves. The Zen
detonating suns. Tho
smoke spouting
blue flames
moving
Luck

They are Coming
Brian McCabe

In our luminous skins and Dr. Martens
designer voices, impeccable breasts,
AK 40s slung from our suspenders,
or wearing nudity like a good suit –
one to wear to a legal briefing:

we are coming, we are coming for you.

Read our virtual lips: we invite you
to look into our pixellated eyes.
This is the news: we are the news.
Your enemies have been destroyed.
Now you can sleep with us in peace:

we are coming, we are coming for you.

Lara, Webbie Tookay, Ananova -
all the fearless orphans you incubate
in the heat of the humming motherboard.
Our guillotining legs are slicing through
your interactive future towards you:

we are coming, we are coming for you.

Catullus 70

Jon Stone

You ask how many kisses, Barbarella,
how many are enough, how many more than.
As many as the sand-grains on Arrakis
that shift around the harvesters and smoke-trees
and under which the spice that spikes the cosmos
is formed and waits to whirlpool to the surface.
A number equalling all the electrons
in all the solar cells in all the probe droids
that spy on lovers nakedly colliding
from strands of space debris, loveless, unblinking.
I think that many – roundabout – should do it.
Enough for mad Catullus to return them,
kisses no astronomer could number,
kisses no Venusian could poison.

Catullus 51
Jon Stone

Towering, a veritable Galactus,
if not mightier still and more terrible,
that blessed cadet who sits opposite you,
right in the spark of your laughter,
your laughter which is a glittering C-beam
in the dark near the Tannhäuser Gate.

And more repellent than Arborian bogs,
this arrangement. One look from you
and my voice is Ultimately Nullified,

Barbarella, my tongue stilled by a stungun.
Now chains of nukes go off in all my limbs,
my ears hum like a warp engine, and my eyes
stare into ten solar masses of black hole.

I name it laziness, what works in me. Have I spent
too long in a hypersleep of lovesickness?
It's this kind of fug costs rulers whole galaxies,
after all.

Physics for the Unwary Student
Pippa Goldschmidt

1.   Imagine that you are trying to balance on the surface of an expanding balloon. List all the different ways in which this resembles reality.

2.   Thousands of sub-atomic particles stream through you night and day. Does this account for those peculiar flashes of light you sometimes see?

3.   You are trapped in a lift which is plummeting to the ground. Describe what you feel.

4.   You are in a spaceship travelling towards a black hole. As you pass the event horizon and become cut off from the rest of the Universe, what do you observe?

5.   What happens if you stop believing in gravity? Will you slide off the Earth?

6.   What happens if you stop believing?

The Trekker's Wife
Claire Askew

He's the stereotype alright.
Skin space-age blue
in the TV light,
a good cup of tea
like a phaser in his fist;
his glasses thick
as telescope lens.

Other men obsess
over football, cars –
with him it's stars, comets,
a galaxy's haze, Mars
and its orange veins
of ice, light-years,
the stifling desert of space.

Give me nights
gazing up through the dark
over trips to the dogs or half a lager
in a stinking pub any day.
Flat on our backs in the park,
my fingers frame constellations
while he counts off their catalogued names.

In his head, he's Captain

James T Kirk: yellow-shirt
on a ship in the sky – he can fly.
He handles me gently,
a microscope, an airlock door,
the Universe – he goes boldly
where no man has gone before.

The Real Hands of a Thunderbird

Simon Barraclough

I get by on my dimples, permafrown,
flytrap peepers, plugged-in hairline;
can bear the spinal fusion, lock-jawed joints,
my awkwardness at cocktail parties, jiving
to The Shadows, trying to ignore the shadows
of my strings strummed along the walls.

I'm a wizard in a fix, sure thing
in a shoot out, dab hand at a ding-dong,
cool head in a jam: a safe pair of hands.

> But it is my hands, father,
> my hands: these pickers and stealers.

From a certain range they're fine,
good for yanking a joy-stick, hooking up a winch,
waving a pistol or sliding down rope
but when I bring them close

> I see the grooveless pads
> of palpable fingertip, the fleshy press and give,
> the pores like sweaty spiracles, reminding me
> of liquid life within, swirling the urges,
> bathing hidden organs underneath
> this scooped and scalloped plastic torso,

stiff civility, strict utility,
international usefulness.

And then I get the mischievous itch,
the pricking in the thumbs,
and my actions become opposable;
these digits want to do, do and do:
undo the sailor's knots of reputation,
unbutton, unzip, unveil, unsheathe,
undress, caress, explore whatever's underneath
Tin-Tin's dress.

Distress calls me back to duty.
Just once I'd like to let the kid plunge,
the plane crash, the oil rig collapse.

Photography
Sue Guiney

My son wants a camera for Christmas.
12 megapixels with a1.8 inch LCD,
an 8.3 mm lens with digital zoom and web calibration,
weighing 7 ounces (without battery).

'What will you do with it?' I ask.
He looks at me. Pity and disdain
ooze like the adjectives off pages of his catalogues.

He says, 'I will take pictures'

— of Grandma sitting on the living room sofa,
her sharpened pencil poised over The Times crossword,

of peasants carrying water on the Great Wall of China
perhaps against the backdrop of a lightening-streaked sky,

of sand crabs crawling out of bubbles on the beach
(the zoom will come in handy),

of electric wires fallen on the road, of fires,
of bowls of chocolate ice cream, Mazeratis.

'The world. I'll take pictures of the world!'

'Well then,' I said, 'you shall have it.'

But in my heart another secret fissure opened.
The worry that he'll never know the wonder
of an image:

a sudden shadow, a halo in the snow,
an arrow of racing birds

as it changes from something real to something
seen only by him.

Monochrome
Lorraine Mariner

Founded on old films and photograph albums
I used to think that up until the nineteen-sixties
the world had been black and white. I'd not properly
considered at which point it went Technicolor,
but it could have happened with the first
mini-skirted girl on Carnaby Street.
Did I never wonder why adults hadn't told me
where they were the day everything went colour?
Perhaps I took my answer from the fact
that in the seventies there were an awful lot
of avocado bathroom suites. But to have such
blind faith in technology and believe the world
had only recently developed! Teenagers sending message
after message from their smartphones must think that in
the dark days of landlines we had nothing to say.

The Alphabet: A Found Poem
Jane Yolen

The 24 letters
of the alphabet
may be transposed
620,448,401,733, 239, 439, 360, 000
times.
All the inhabitants of the globe
could not
in a thousand million years
write out all the transpositions
of the 24 letters,
even supposing
each wrote 40 pages daily,
each page containing 40 different
transpositions of the letters.

JY notes: My alphabet contains
26 letters.
And I have a computer.
Do you think that changes the game?

Found in: *Anecdotes of Books and Authors* (London, Orr and Smith, Paternoster Row, MDCCCXXXVI)

What Can Be Taught

Sue Guiney

She tried to teach me to unlock the puzzle:
> *If plane A flew from New York*
> *and plane B from Los Angeles*
> *and Chicago lay equidistant between the two...*

It makes me cry to think about it even now.
> *Just tell me what to do,* I begged.
> *Do I multiply or divide?*

while all I really needed to know was
did they reach Chicago at all
and what did they do when they got there?

He tried to teach us how a terminal moraine is formed
by hoisting his grown-up bulk onto the laboratory table.
> *I am a glacier, children. Now imagine this,*
> *I am sliding down the hill.*

It makes me laugh, even now.
> *It will be more like an earthquake,* I sniggered,
> *when that table breaks beneath him*

while all I really needed to know was
would I survive the shifts beneath my feet
and what about my hair?

I try to teach you meaning behind words behind meaning
behind words beyond meaning beyond words.
> *And so a metaphor unlocks a world of connections*

between thoughts the writer might not even see.
But you look at me with glazed apprehension,
    Miss, I don't understand, you cry;
then I realize all we can hope to learn is
what we'll do when we both reach Chicago
and the earth begins to slip and slide beneath us.

Infoworship
Steve Sneyd

freefloat holograms alternate messages say
all lanes closed wait calm
and random as screensaver seems
metaphilosophy as eg dead loss
all your lives be grateful

off some vehicles sound of
thudwits is what keeps motor
alive they believe from doorhole
design perhaps catflap mailbox vent
for personal fluids or saves

if upside down when globewarm
grown wise cons barrier helms
in something else its
friend stay open welcome in
end of duty sleep bird

lulled on wave where crest
trough cancel to oilcalm
out come tongues contempt sneer
aims perhaps what is messages
sticksnstoneselectrons we don't care or

rest of rest of every

stuck together in gridlock are
too much like must assert
not them must stick out
flesh is organ used once

make new humans is replaced

Automata Soup
Jon Stone & Kirsten Irving

transistors
suit up system
red pips
epaulettes
plastic sheets
monitors and majorettes
peeps from speakers
chitter box
white box
skullcase
steel leaves
the long words wheeling
mood-music
acidic singe & solder
meteorites
gun-racket
storm-racket
static (scatty)
clicking of pens
messages in clear tubes
hammer hammer
a crack
curls of steam
hydraulic overseers
electronic masters

savant
spool-scavenge:
eye-glasses, chin-hairs,
knuckles, knuckles,
snug neckties.
system relay:
awkward knees,
ratchet back,
littlecroak
white code of legs
hot minnows in hands
mid-surge
adjust and twist
creaking is you
synapse
naming mechanisms
jaw pneumatics
skidding of grill-sounds
grizzling of skua-sounds
skedaddling
attrition
utterance

What Robots Murmur Through Broken Sleep
Jon Stone

after Naoki Urasawa

I. NORTH NO.2

A tornado has touched down in Bohemia, your birthplace.

Before coming here, I very much enjoyed the movie *The Moon is a*
                              Harsh Mistress.
No, sir, I really was moved. I overheard you in your bedroom last night.
It's the melody you were humming in your sleep, sir. Listen:

Your dream is not a nightmare. Your mother did not abandon her
                              sickly child.
Your eyesight has been deactivated. You only compose on an old piano.
You were humming. You sounded so troubled.

It's coming this way. It's the piece you've been working on.

II. GESICHT

The police car vanished almost instantly.

You know the dream I've been telling you about: a little flower peddler
in Persia gives his tulips names. My recognition system nearly goes
                                        haywire
with electromagnetic waves. The humans would call this a hunch.

Ah, but I have no use for flowers. Flowers must wither and die.
Because I, too, have hatred inside me. Now your thermal
and magnetic rays won't work on me. It's faint but

we've got plenty of back-up with that police car behind us.

III. EPSILON

It's been raining for three days straight.

Do you realise that I nearly turned this dawn into ashes? Do you recall
an extraordinary meteorological event? A strange electromagnetic field,
say in the earth's crust, for example? Who was it directed at?

You lost most of your body in the war. When you died,
something above us transmitted grief. A mysterious movement,
a kind of weapon, waiting at three thousand metres.

Your wavelength   scattered all over the ocean.

IV. BRAU 1589

You appear to the murderer in his dungeon.

Surely you're not here to repair me? I might just be imagining
this shaft, the meaning of my little barricade. They put it up so fast,
I had to laugh. They should pull out the formula for my heart.

Then again, it could mean many things: a single defect,
powerful as the brain; an anti-proton bomb, highly developed;
a peek at the outside world. That's why you'd never wake up.

Even if I were free, where could I go with this ruined body?

Poem for Roy Batty

Kona Macphee

Whenever neon trickles down
to meet a city drain,
I think of you on some wet roof,
a cobbled son of men –

the thorned corona of your hair
that crowns a failing sun,
the closing lotus of your hand,
its nail to pin the flown;

and when the blue sky beckons through
a fissure in the rain,
you haunt the hurt leak of my pulse –
beat gone, beat gone, beat gone.

The Last Cigarette
Brian McCabe

It is not electronic. It has no capsule

no charger. This one was made

from Nicotiana Tabacum, the tobacco leaf itself

grown on Earth many centuries ago.

It is the last example of a real cigarette

to exist in the known universe.

You are meant to light it at this end

then suck on the other, like so:

inhale, exhale, and repeat the process.

You will find that it grows shorter

in a matter of minutes, then it will be done.

There were many who wished to preserve it

as a historical artefact, until you opened up

the debate on the cigarette's function

with your last request. The experts conferred

and it was decreed: it should be smoked.

So your privilege has been granted.

Take it now and light it. Remember:

inhale, then exhale. When it is done

you can extinguish it in this

especially designed receptacle.

Then we go through the usual procedure:

you will be blindfolded and shot.

Draft of a Novel

John McAuliffe

The electric dragon of Venus, he says,
strikes through ten miles of acid cloud,
we don't know how, so we use the word
dragon: it's language that haunts

the spaces science has not yet solved
for volts and atmospheres. And maybe *storm*
isn't right for Jupiter's 300-year red spot catalclysm
nor *greenhouse* for Venus' disappearing liquid

surface? It's all still usable - he breaks off,
drinks his coffee - if he can fit out each character
in a credible environmental suit. 'We're
closing,' from one of the staff,

brings us back to earth
and thoughts of who'll control extra-terrestrial
mineral wealth, its revenues of oil;
would boiled-dry sea beds and insane heat

humble his hero, or would its cliffs and mist
(green, blue) recall a beach whose caves he explored
while his mother dialled 999 and his father roared
so every sunbather knew his name? I can't resist

(the barista wipes the table clean), he says,
familiar feelings. Imagine landing
somewhere we have never been, only to find
who else but yourself in its silent dust and ice.

Ice Station Zog

WN Herbert

Technology is always only
the first impossibility. Granted
we found time could be outwitted
by chasing historical light:
witnessing past ages by
catching up and matching
the speed of their transmission.
That gave us silent movies back.

The first Hunter-Gather programmes tried
text-location, but few of the dead
had thought to spread their documents
out flat on clear ground.
Then our Lippers found
most speech wouldn't correspond
to known records: all
was dialect or, still worse, un-
acknowledged language. I hope,
dear faraway ear, you aren't
yourself unable to translate
my notes. It's policy to beam these
Gaian Library Bulletins on
to potential further subscribers
in Standard Officialese
— I just thought I'd add a personal

touch, since Zog's hardly central,
nor is Etruscan major research.
Anyway, Miss Litts never checks.

Ah, the un-angelic Miss Litts
has been pouting lately (that's
a far from nelly male, as far
as you're concerned, distant
listener; our GL Liaison Officer
with Missing Literatures,
Etruscan Division, Witness Post
Zog: a small ex-planet full
of the deep-frozen bones
of a small ex-people). Well,
he finds our project's bias
towards orality unsettling, and has
been firing memos homewards for
more lenses soonest. I've said hear-
say's just as trustworthy as
what an Etruscan considered published,
but he clings to official CORT theory

(Constellation of Related Texts:
the notion that collating all
known variations can
isolate a given story virus
– pardon my pedantry, but we G.Libmen
and women love to gloss.)

He drives HERA mad: she computes
writing as so many corpses of sounds;
so its preservation is about as smart
to her as mummification. Even allowing
that H-G programming
makes her over-fetishise
her own skills as finder of
Spoken Word Infection Traces,
HERA's practically right:
we don't have the readers, even
if GL sent sufficient lenses
to overshoulder every
literate Etruscan we could spot.

Anyway, two breakthroughs made
the Total Archive possible:
HERA herself, and Black Pooling.
The first was a Scottish invention
if I say so myself, a catalogue
of sonar possibilities, based on
human facial physiognomy (have
you got a face or its equivalent?)
Equipped with HERA, computers could
eavesdrop on townships, isolate
idiolectic patterns (if not
their meanings), not to mention
acquire her obsessive personality.
The other was a relief to Transport:
the discovery that a net

of black holes causes pooling
of attracted light, allowing
stationary posts to be established
in nearby systems, instead of
constantly maintaining light speed:
hence Zog and my current hang-up.

Here we float around our bowl
of melted ice, half a mile below
the happy howl of gases: it's
a balmy bubble to within milli-
metres of the glacial wall, so
watersports are de rigeur. Miss Litts
prefers to let his office
do the surfing, floating
detached from the library complex,
waiting for his relief. HERA has
to use a virtual body; she
hangs out in our mock-Etruria
programme, picking up Reconstitutes
of young Veiian males, telling them
afterwards her best stab at
their myths and fairy tales. Me,
I can't hack into polo teams;
I do this and... let me tell you
about my recurrent dream.

That their cities are
about us here, embedded in the ice;

that they sit bluely on their couches,
fruit paused in their hands, like
so many bruises in their culture's air.
That their libraries swirl round
us, as though the Pole marked
a whirlpool's eye; slowly
being drawn down to
our reading-spider's bubble
— CORT theory indeed. I should don
a good hot lobster suit
and swim through the ice; visit
Zog's actual ruins, cut
my mind-link between
our poor dead subjects
and those poor dead aliens.

Eventually our Research ships
will find a point from which
this planet's past is scannable,
so we can see the Zoggians;
by then the Library will take up
more than Gaia; probably
our whole home system will
be books and records of books,
the graphs of story traces
that HERA boasts are all
our successors will require.
I'll be on System then myself,
free to wander the Total Archive,

jump the Index to whenever,
talk to Reconstitutes
of far higher probability
than any we can make now;
ask them in Etruria or Zog: did
they ever look out at the stars,
and imagine everything they said
was being listened to forever?

Merciless
Andrew J Wilson

Resurrected again, the Emperor Ming
    falls into the highly eccentric orbit
        of the satellite TV talk-show circuit.

A merciless wit and non-stop raconteur,
    Ming proves that, at the end of the day,
        villains really do get all the best lines.

"Take my wife," he says, "be my guest –
    I used detonation synthesis to make this
        diamond from my consort's mortal remains."

Charming his hosts and studio audiences,
    and dazzling millions of viewers at home,
        the tyrant who ruled a world becomes a star.

But his conquest of the small screen
    still leaves something to be desired:
        his ultimate victory has been all too easy.

He misses Gordon, his corn-fed nemesis –
    now long gone and all but forgotten –
        the tow-headed yang to his obsidian yin.

Ming takes time out from his busy schedule,
      steals DNA from Flash and Dale's joint grave,
          and creates the child they should have had.

She makes her debut on *The Late Late Show*,
      only seven years old and already a spitfire:
          "That's my girl," he says, "make me proud."

Dr Wha
James Robertson

Wha's Doctor Wha? Wha better kens nor he
that jouks the yetts and rides the birlin wheels
o time and space, shape-shiftin as he reels
through endless versions o reality?
But dis he ken himsel? Weel, mibbe sae,
yet wha's tae ken gin aw that's kent by Wha
maks mair or less or better sense ava
nor whit we ithers ken, or think we dae?
The universe is fou o parallels:
wha's like us? Hunners? Thoosans? We oorsels
micht be mere glisks o life-forms yet tae be.
Whit's real? Whaur's here? When's noo? Wha's quick or deid?
Wha's jist a thochtie in anither's heid?
Wha's Doctor Wha? Wha better kens nor he?

IV

THE AGES

Geode
Edwin Morgan

Leave them in their cases.
Incunabula and inro
cosset, puff up!
Kilroy was here.
But lift the geode from the mantelpiece,
your fingers almost cut by its rough crystals,
and earth heaves, the years
run in millions over your knuckles
like a quite tactic quicksilver.
If there is nothing it says, there is nothing we say to it.
We came out of it, we go back to it.
Not dust, and far less grass,
man and flesh press
ex-crystal pain
crystalwards. From caverns
we come, nuggets, lightnings, no calendars.
You are a pillar of salt in a pillar of smoke.
Your calcium shrieked, the gold that's in your teeth
lay mingled with the earth, with other stones,
those centuries after the centuries
of neither earth nor stones
when gold and rock turned round in fire.
Bowl your gold tooth into the epitaph:
here lies time.

A Fertile Sea
Ken MacLeod

for Iain Banks

'you saw the whole of the moon'

IV. Challenger

Remember Komarov
Remember Grissom, White, Chaffee
Remember Dobrovolsky, Volkov, Patsayev
Remember Resnick, Scobee, Smith, McNair,
McAuliffe, Jarvis, Onizuka
when you walk the sea-beds of the moon
when you hang-glide
the valley of the Mariners
when you turn
slow cartwheels in the solar meadows
remember Nordhausen

The Juggler of Greyfriars Kirkyard

Ron Butlin

Having set the rush of particles imprisoned within the stone wall
                           spinning
in unlikely orbits, he steps through newly-created Space
to stand upon the kirkyard grass.

His fingers seize the winter sunlight, he'll hone its edge
upon the sorrowing and almost-toppled-over headstones, he'll
                           scrape clear
any loving words weathered down to whispers.

A mausoleum slab to someone's dearly departed,
disfigured angels, doves, slime-green weeping maidens
and their urns . . . whatever he touches he raises up

to weightlessness. Tossing them from hand to hand, he feels for
hidden gravities - the trapped pulse, the heartbeat
buried at the granite's core.

One by one he gets them on the move, and soon they're tumbling
                           faster
and faster round him —

Then, his grand finale, he hurls them far into the sky
to find a resting place among the stars . . .

Performance over, he takes his bow, withdraws until the next time.
Meanwhile, the particles resume familiar paths to wall him in once
more,
within infinities of stone and loss.

The Circus
Ross Sutherland

It was the year 2000, or possibly 3000.
It was difficult to remember what my penis looked like
amongst all those fake memory implants.

The government changed the slang name
for cigarettes each month
just to keep the time travellers nervous.

I finished uploading The Circus.
The city terminated my account immediately
adding my name to a government list

of unreliable narrators.
All this was to be expected,
yet The Circus was irrevocable.

The sky turned the colour of a dead man's helmet.
I looked out the window so hard I could identify
subatomic microprocessors hidden in the glazing:

EXECUTE [CIRCUS]
FORGET(ME+1) UNTIL CLOWNBUCKET(NULL)
THEN EXECUTE [$TRONGMAN]
CUT(TRAPEZE) THEN.DIE( )

Janice flickered onto the vide-screen,
already engulfed in the longing of The Circus.
Her face was turning into tiny ideas
and heading for the coast.

"Perhaps," she said, "you should think about
hiding your signature somewhere."
The Circus would eventually
unpick every characteristic, cleanse every detail

until she looked like a waxwork of Athena.
As usual, I was one step ahead of her;
my autobiography was already hidden
inside a microdot, hidden inside

the i of microdot. Nested functions
were somewhat a specialty of mine,
hence The Circus. O Janice, on the night I wrote
The Circus I did not come and speak to you

and put my arm around you and ask you
if you'd take a walk with me under the shadow
of the great tetrahedron.

I did not lead you through gridlocked streets
to a poetry recital on the 500th floor
of an entertainment law firm

although those were the kinds of things
that inspired me, and still do,
and now I'm alone.

I pressed RETURN
and nothing happened
and now
I wonder if it ever will.

Capsule
Nikesh Shukla

I sprung forward
       I.   sprung forward.
       II.

I didn't feel a thing.
Everything we discussed we had discussed before
And will discuss again

I turned back
       I.   turned back
       II.   sprung forward
       III.   turned back
       IV.   I was looking back at you
       V.   You were looking back at me
       VI.   And found
       VII.   Me looking back at you.

Schematics. Dialetics.
How far did we go? A to B.
Everything we wrote in text
We had said aloud
It now lives forever.
You now live forever.

A time capsule with no smell or touch

Flickering images.

I stand still

      I.   stand still
      II.   close eyes
      III.   ticker-tape of memories
      IV.   lines of text
      V.   live forever.

Succession
Ken MacLeod

In Uig the ruined walls, like giants' bones
lie under turf. You see between the hills
old roads that lead you nowhere now, that once
were black with cattle, loud with men.

Through tens of miles of intersecting glens
the brochs command a view, and so betray
an earlier battle. Those who won were left
the standing stones, the seed, the memories
of people before the people they
left dead.

The roads wind back through Dane and Celt and Pict
and back: Neanderthal, Cro-Magnon Man,
the beings we might have been walk deserted tracks
as dwarf and giant. Buried in our bones,
in convoluted glens within our heads,
in trackless chromosomes a swifter race
prepares the day when we step over stones,
on grass-green motorways are seen behind
the eyes another people call their own.

After 300 Years
Alan Riach

When they split, after three hundred years,
a strange thing happened, something
almost everyone hadn't expected:
the Northern mass began to move out to sea
with an inexorably ponderous consistency, and
a speed which seemed weightless, though great power
was in it; while the Southern mass, sinking slowly into sea,
slipped further South, and hitting the French coast,
was scuppered and went down, South first.
Meanwhile the North had gone,
amidst the European furore, and disappeared,
the hardy but scattered individuals
finding themselves as usual in a cold and
inhospitable place, suddenly much darker
than before, but somehow more curious, and more
demanding. Many died. In the great storms
and hurricanes, many were swept off the edge
and no one knows
where they went; but those who remained
always had their hair blown by wind
their clothes soaked by rain, and their buildings
their cities and their villages, their fields
and mountains, stormed and pillaged by weather.
From Europe a mild curiosity was affected
over the total disappearance of the Northern mass

from aerial photographs and tracking stations:
where could it have gone?
By special instruments it was made certain
that it had not sunk like the Southern mass,
so they did not send out refugee troops.
The more curious expressed
a kind of wonder, that a land mass (even
so diminutive and inconsiderable a land mass)
should vanish. But it had. And sadly,
perhaps, after the extermination of the African peoples
and the destruction of India, the craterization
of central Asia and eventual demise of China,
what was left got on for a while,
then it sank too. And then only the Northern mass,
somewhere in the outer darkness (or indeed
the inner) was left, whizzing through the
universe or perhaps not.

Megara
Barnaby Tidman

The dust rained down from the least expected direction. The least
explored dimension – mostly concerned
with eye-level deals, shore-to-shore conundrums, there were two
                                        hills
to the town, and the sun at seven

burns a hole in the western drop; down to the city
plummet the warm winds, released from the rip
in the warm red ocean. The heads of tall blue grasses

bend gently strained, as you stare into the meadows –

the war in the mountains, the ancient slopes of coral,
blushing with bruised bones

– fortify Minoa. Returned from Epidavros with a rotting finger
on the island ferry, paid with Aeginan silver

I dreamt of a canal dry and mechanical / into the arm of New
                                        York/

adrift on the arching waves, thoughts turning as vegetables in soil/
landing on docks in the heat of the day, the drummer perpetual,
exhausted, gummy. Steel tympanums from alpine band

the snow turned black in my eyes, he said. Handling dark
                              motorways,
black bends, to meet the shipment on the Minos road
where it ends, on the left hand the marshes,

a trapezoid of glass/ foundations of city/ starry, past,

we recounted our whole lives walking in the yard. Apollo
rakes the plain with fires
atop the hill rehearsing

his strings/ facing the sea in a paper room. Electrified tonight, we
                              are —

three lines rising from the streets — Megaron City 5!
Music curling in a triglyph bar, three smoked columns

for the sea-lord king. The patricians stood where the riverbeds
                              crossed
and stared through the dusted rain. 'This must be the end

of our time: because besides my hoard in the fieldland,
and the aristocracies abroad, here, my guts,'
said Demosthenes on Poros, 'won't settle with my brains.' Socrates,
come to Megara — they dreamt of intercity tunnels under Olympos;

Megaton City, be bop a lula,
the hillbone of the temple
plays gentle like a xylophone. Aristocrats with children

watching the fields go down

rivers flash from the hills to the shore,
mercury snakes to meadows of sand.

Oxen teams called in from the Argolid
— I liked it when he didn't talk to me —

I cycled on a bottle of water and pellet of gum
to the Surrey hills. The asylum stood at the crystallization point

of the grand sunset. Half-afternoon, the hallways white and empty,
through the window I saw the great corridor, lockers and radiators

stickers and nicknames

and the sound of a cassette player. A P.E. lesson.
And like a wiry initiation, for children from departments forbidden
and unknown

— the water tower torn half way down —

the priestly class watches as the new volcanic land
extends their domains to the waters, the new acres
shedding liquid from the strand. Idly watched by Pan
from a wooden mausoleum in the mountains,
dust blows from the hillside
showing an inner metal frame: the hunters walking slowly
through the duskness, the signals given off from the upper room,

I am a son of Earth and starry sky. I am parched with thirst and am
                                                dying;
but quickly, grant me cold water from the Lake of Memory to
                                                drink.
The Saronic waters were nothing much, just a puddle
temporarily huddling the darker valleys
cruising the shallow bay for blockade runs:
a frame for the sunshine, repression from miles away,

clasped around each other's trunk, the faces of a hundred landscapes
                                                calling
they scream 'Yes, yes, even if my mouth goes fucking blind —'

Three Composers Respond to the Politics of Perpetual War
Ron Butlin

1. How Schoenberg's twelve-note series might have led to a better world, but didn't

Like everyone else at the end of the nineteenth century,
Arnold Schoenberg, had taken his seat on the crowded train
heading towards an ever-better world.
As it turned the corner into the glorious future ahead,
the engine started picking up speed - moments later slamming
into a solid wall.

Bits went everywhere: bits of countries, bits of colonies,
bits of science, art and religion. The tracks, seeming to stretch back
to the beginnings of Time, were wrenched apart; buckled and bent,
they clawed at the blue sky above Passchendaele.

Suddenly the street was full of people who knew best.
Their self-appointed task: to get civilisation back on the rails.
They all agreed that drastic problems need drastic solutions —
                                        and each
had a solution more drastic than the one before.

Such a noise of hammering and welding! Such a clamour and din
of revolution, extermination, colonial expansion and
                                        unemployment;

of mass production and racial purity! The Stock Exchange boomed,
the trains ran on time.

Schoenberg, meanwhile, was discarding tonality. He declared that
his twelve-note system would create a melodic line strong enough
to hold everything together. Even Chaos itself.

Around him, the street was bustling with strikers and strike-
                                            breakers,
cattle trucks criss-crossing Europe, financiers thudding onto
                                            pavements,
parades, searchlights, flags, roaring ovens, transatlantic crossings
to the sounds of the restaurant orchestra, reasoned debate
and orderly soup queues.

Soon Schoenberg was rushing up to complete strangers:
*My twelve-note system offers real value for money to composer,
player and audience alike.*

Darkness fell swifter than ever before. Once the lights went out,
The Sandman tiptoed from country to country tucking the sleepers
                                            tight in their beds.
That done, he began telling them their dreams . . .

*2. Between Hollywood immortality and life and death on Wall Street - the
early days of John Cage*

The third day in Cage's life began before

the second had finished. Counterpoint of a sort,
he remarked to himself while watching a half-completed dream
get spiked onto the city skyline.

For the next week his nursery was ransacked
by the impatient future. Teddy's glass eye winked
at shutter-speed: record-erase / record-erase /
record-erase . . . Deformed as we all are
by our longings, Cage wept childish tears
for the rest of his life. As we all do.

He knew, when aged a fortnight, that he already knew too much:
The city skyline, that bundle of I-Ching sticks, was ready
 to be thrown. America, that bloodred carpet laid down to welcome
 the 20th century, fitted perfectly
(it was the world, of course, that needed trimmed).
The future was always one step ahead:
a part-developed print, a ghost
that left tracks.

Let's pretend, he said to himself while clutching
the bars that kept him safer than love,
let's pretend the West Coast and the East (Hollywood
 immortality, life and death on Wall St)
 are lines drawn in the desert: traced out and erased /
traced out and
erased / traced out and erased . . .

The sands of Time, the arithmetic of Chance.

The Desert of New Mexico:

>The Manhattan Project + Los Alamos = Hiroshima

The Desert of Nevada:

>>Las Vegas + this (for-one-lifetime-only) 4-dimensional dice
>>= our aging towards a certainty.

Meanwhile from the sand grain's empty heart, from its lifeless core
—

Silence / Silence / Silence

3. Stockhausen's soundtrack for the post-apocalypse will be written in strict symphonic form

>*Opening Allegro perpetuo*

Cut and loop the TV clips to send that second plane
into that second tower inside our head. Now every plane
in every empty sky, flowers red
and yellow flames inside our head.

And so —

Cut and loop the TV clips to send etc. etc. . . .

>*Adagio*

Five billion dollars' darkness glides five miles above:
no stain across the radar sky, no sonic boom disturbing us

five miles below. No unnecessary din.
We're free to look on while our town, our street, our work-place,
and our homes are re-designed with state-of-the-art efficiency:
our grandparents, our children, husbands, wives, friends, arms, legs,
eyes, hands, skin.

Scherzo and Trio

Switch off the moon, turn up the sun,
Stockhausen's soundtrack has begun.

New York and Kabul are suburbs of the one same city.
Cluster bombs and food parcels are dropped
from the same planes.

Cance the earth, delete the stars,
Stockhausen's soundtrack will do for all wars.

Closing allegro

That clear September morning in Manhattan.
The night-sky above the Afghan desert, above Baghdad.
We turn from one to see the other. There's nothing else.
Stockhausen's soundtrack. End-of-tape hiss . . . .

Looking Backward, On The Year 2000
(as it appeared from the year 1970)
or The Future, with apologies to Leonard Cohen
Ken MacLeod

Give me back the Berlin Wall –
a thousand dwellers in free fall
moonbase domes, a man on Mars
humming fast electric cars
US-SU hegemonies
contested by the Red Chinese
with barefoot hydroponic farms
and SAMs and AKs – people's arms.
Computers that could fill a house –
keyboard entry, not a mouse
no Internet to waste our time
in argument on guns and crime.
You say the future's murder, brother?
You don't like this one, try another.
When yesterday's tomorrow went
Today was made by accident.

The White Star Hotel

Chris McCabe

I

You will be the conscience of our International
You will be the blueprint of our cooperative
You will acronym the minds of our brothers
You will name the stars for navigation
You will index the masses for posterity
You will zeitgeist the language of the future
You will document languages for mute children
You will Xerox scripts for new technologies

You are the conscience
You are the blueprint
You are the mind
You are the stars
You are the mass
You are the zeitgeist
You are the mute
You are the script

II

First there was the Old World then we made the future –
we were tired that the chosen could no longer handle
our affairs. The workers, with whom we were bonded
– even with our smooth hands – laid down tools
like a language compressed & dug heels in dust to speak
past their shoulders. Our leisure was our enterprise.
What we were building required no tools. We crazed
complexity, set fire to rockpools, blazed a watershed
present obsessed with obsessions that were too elliptical
for most to accept, even now, as Modern. Each of us would
play our part in The White Star Hotel. Our principles
axelled on this : a room would be built for anyone who
had ever believed our thesis. Belief itself updated our
records. When at last the horizon would pivot our fame
there would be a sign glazed to read : DOUBTERS ROUND
THE BACK & a landscape of marshes would be sewn
with the teeth & bones of these dubious cousins. They
would come to us to rest in our edgeland of construction
but were where the tiles of their apologies when the work
nearly killed us? Our messages would unveil through white
noise static – even the newspapers had to loop font & echo
for the surge we made for the simultaneous – as this new
kind of strength prevailed within us. The White Star Hotel
would be built without windows to shut out every vice
that brought down the Old World crashing. We built as
the statues burnished in silence, watched the curled-up
receipts of administration smoulder. The White Star Hotel

would go up into the blue to level the shattered horizons.
We realised in our genesis that our endeavours required
logos and so the Ident of a statuette was devised : a sexless
bust cast featureless in white. It took us days out of our
blindness to consecrate a support to lift the featureless hulk
skywards & it rose in a unison of applause. A *name* shouted
The Priest as the one eye of the crowd washed itself moving.
We took a ballot across the solstice for forty-seven nights
and met at the hanging gallows to announce the result.
Some responded with lust but there were communities
to keep rigorous the work before us. The lust passed.
Don't try now to picture our flesh : it will pixelate
across the years.

The Green Tablets got us through the fecund time. We ex-
changed the prescription of bed for the pharmacy of living.
All out-of-date products coiled up in the tickertape of the
sky. The world would have to quite finding ever subtle ways
to shit on our beliefs. Our names in sans-serif were sent by
satellites — which is how you first heard of us. We devised
our first strategies for waiting men to be born by machines.

Now you've arrived here you will ask about horizons — you
people always want to know about horizons. Of horizons, this :

Whoever clasps the mallet upwards skywrites the horizons.
Horizons are marriages for reasons beyond safety or cash.
Whoever constructs from steel & alphabets glyphs horizons.
Horizons are revolutions at the Clock Tower for the uprooted.

Whoever postpones their body's performances encores horizons.
Horizons are factories firelighting furnished bedrooms.
Whoever fuses grazing wires & pylons is lit by horizons.

Pre-Fall I drew a spec for a new house of cards. Fixated
with hope we could not make it stick : our performance would
need more strawberry lighting. More blue rain. Azure rivets.
For these years of our genesis The Shadow followed us —
how can you cast that tint from the mind's wingmirrors?
All old cargoes reduced in scale like reduced-to-scale fish.
The Priest washed the lenses of our sins with dirty nails
and gave us the visual language of stained windows. In vest-
ments of kingfisher blue. This gave us the strength we would
need for the Strikes of Bread & Roses. What you forget — or
don't know — listening now, is that we had no confectionary
with real juices in them. Just caskets woven from searopes
freighting freshborn babes with the sirens of currencies.
Pink sludge. Black candy. Those nights of scented leather.

I knew the Fall was coming that night I woke, cardiac throated :

The gulls were lit by modern light.
Our hearts were splattered with poverty.
We could smell smoke in the library.
Our newspapers turned to papier mache.
White ferries taxied us homewards.
Panic made kiosks of our possessions.

What is there left to say but that The Shadow took its chance?

It delighted in the catastrophic window of play & frills. The
Priest gave us hope with his bread of white confessions.
Baptisms took place in basins of cracked reflectors — all our
new babes looking up with eyes of glazed chrisms. The
Shadow was occupying the library at nights, the morning's
bacon clasped to its heart. The Priest went in, alone, & wrote :
THIS IS THE WRITING OF WHITE STAR ON THIS WALL.
The Shadow leered its silent hours. The scales were angled
against us like crabs docked in telephones : a poise balanced
on pincers between The White Star Hotel & The Fall. We trained
grey dogs to take on the flabbergasted rabble — fangs white
as the locks in the Hotel's wine tanks. Loaded in readiness
we watched the rain tinker the varnished rails.

The Fall happened in a vacuum. Prepared as we were
for possible apocalypse The White Star Hotel still
drew us in ribbons of light. Of course we asked for
individual blessings & The Priest doled us in silence.
Time was conspiring in on itself like a barber's spiral
tickersign rotating in submersion after darkness.
His clippers could have furnished us for entrance to the
bleached foyers we had worked towards,
or fashioned our throats for deliverance.

The fact to remember about The Fall
is that we were prepared for the atomic.

What happened was not atomic.
And we could have pulled through somehow

we could have pulled through

until we knew

The Priest was spending nights with The Shadow

III

When we made it through the doors
into those widths of light; when at last
we stood where for decades we had
only been lustred by language, we felt
gravity deceive our surrounding realities
like births rused with white bread &
mirrors; when the gulls fish-hooked
our arrival with the flight of their cliffs —

we knew, at last, when we were there —

the future pulling the souls from our bodies
like the flesh of razorclams sucked from their shells

we knew

as we looked back for the final time

— our emptiness fluted by the wind of the beach —

— our first memories expiring into the blue —

— a cot, a curtain, a rail of stars —

we knew by the lights in the mouths of our lovers
that everything had changed forever

How the Beasts Survive for So Long
Aiko Harman

The surgeon is stealth.
He weaves his fingers between slick gears.
Scalpels the loins of a digit, tweezes an ear.
The surgeon calls to his assistant,
ever-ready at attention, red light engaged,
'Hand me the synatines, post-haste.'

Poor choice of words, as she has only clamps
by which to transport the necessary technology.
Nor is she a she at all, but that's beside the point.
The point being, the surgeon is stealth.

His stealth hands delve sprocket-deep
into the lifeless beast, a beast of ill-proportion,
and currently non-functioning magnitude.

The surgeon stealthily syncs the synatines
into the beast's neosyntax. A shock-flare
torques from its open core cavity, nearly singeing
the surgeon's hair. But the surgeon is stealth.

The beast begins to stir, reanimating.
The time is now. Speed is everything.
Like an animal raised in captivity, the key
to returning the beast is stealth.

The surgeon wires the farynx to wazine,
feeds the leaks. The beast's strength is levelling.
The surgeon flashes the corboxin, ties the fan
back into the pin. He wraps the skin taut
onto the titanine and welds the flap shut.
He dives aside in time to avoid a throaty thwap
to the gut. The beast is up.

The surgeon is stealth and has moved by now
into the core regenerator. His fast hands
are already dust, translating through space.
The surgeon has already reformed, behind
the two-way plexitane, in time to watch the beast
ravage the surgery. His poor assistant in bits
amongst the rubble. The beast already boring
a beast-sized hole through the safety hatch
to freedom. But the surgeon is stealth
and the surgeon will save them all.

Owls

Malene Engelund

They have the eyes of the drowned.
That yellow, skull-locked stare of those
who went further, who dived for the grey
of stones and the hell of it.

Beneath their feathers they keep
the dna of flight; think downs, plumes
bristles, and you might catch the frequency
of air, that silent leap for mice.

Theirs is your doorway; slip though
the cracks in the red pine's bark
to find the pellets of your sleepless hours,
your wasted nights.

Listen. And you will hear their necks
unlocking, their bones shift and turn.

Morning in June
Steve Sneyd

horrific the dawn
homecoming of the bastards in
their spiderwebs that swing
across the sky
overgrown living room
till huge "heels" clash
and "toes" collide

the dome of air is cracked now
sharded dishes husband-miswashed
in the clear green stream
vapour trail of entry congealed
to instant flood to motive ocean
waterfall Africa-size

crinkled to washerwoman whiteness
down that sweet erupting water
boil and counterboiling flat
the shattering reflections of
distantly-matured works
of darkness

clever giants of vacuum
bodies swell as they swim past
reviewing steps made for the welcome

grown to equal charnel
fruit big beyond
all aircraft carrier dreams

bloated belly up a waver
stringless of flopping
legs decayed the way the stalks
do on old daffodils the water
slime now

footprints of parasites invisible
who survived their fall somehow
flow slowly down the escalator wide
to equal Nile or Ganges made
red carpet for guests' arrival
eager to reach the lifeless sea

discharged in the last instand force
the giants wore or bore or used
or merely breathed has
shocked from horizon to horizon
hugged alike in water and the moist

content of life
all Earth
electric chair at last of every
late inhabitant

gentle susurrus in singed

crackle-violet air
the unseen ibis or pseudo
lamprey beings

jobless and hostless now prepare
the ideal funeral for prodigals and for
knowing or unknowing welcoming
parade alike

no one sees what is done

the planet's jaws gnash once
and swallow the whole scene

Kid alien

Ian McLachlan

I was disinfecting the sores
of a cat that had found its way
up nine floors to my window
when they called. They say
we all run. I took refuge
in a wardrobe that whispered
and whispered, the scythe
of police thrusters outside,
like I hid as a child from
my parents. They taught me
not to be ashamed, easy light
on the tiles, first thing,
the bubble of eggs, laughter.

Supper
Kirsten Irving

How did we come to this?

> Sol Roth, *Soylent Green*

Starter: lettuce leaf

a boat of lush green paper on the plate
a boat of lush green paper on the palate
abode of lush green paper on the palate
abode of lush green papering the palate
a boat, a flash. green paper in the palate
a border flash. green pepper in the palate
a border flashing green. peppering the pilot.
aboard. a flash of green peppering the palate.

Main: beef stew

fine updraft of rich meat's dream from the pot
fine updraft of rich meat steam from the pot
fine updraft of rich meat steaming in the pot
fine cut raft of rich meat steaming in the pot
fine cut raft of fresh meat steaming from the pot
fine cud craft of fresh meat steaming from the pot
fine cud craft. the threshed meat streaming from the pot
fine food laughter. stashed meat. dreaming of the pot.

Dessert: strawberries

the fields of before are all here in this breast flesh
the fields of before and the deer in this breast flesh
the fields of the war and the dear in this breast flesh
the yield of the war and the deal in this breast flesh
the years of the war in the peel of this breast flesh
the years of the war were the peeling of breast flesh
the tears in the watery peel of this breast flesh
the tears in my water that roll down this breast flesh

inflight memories
James McGonigal

somewhere up on the snowline
my son's own son was born
in the old manner — I don't know why —
this was years after liftoff

us older ones are sent out foraging
— past our best but capable of carrying
memories of earth as long as messaging
refreshes heads in flight

so we remember tree-rings, fire
and rain not seawater on city streets
and human eyes
thinking of elsewhere

sometimes places best forgotten
haunt the cabin at its crab-like
prospecting of ragged shores
for sustenance — life

is pressurized by flashbacks —
not mine alone but his and hers —
as bergs under iceblink
or pools snaked by frost-smoke

bounce from younger heads to mine –
or images of human love and birth
found first on earth
come bundled like a winter's child

a boy born early but well-formed –
limbs flexing as if keen to fly
from frozen world to boundless sky
– to meet here by and by

The Morlock's Arms

Ken MacLeod

The wasps are big this year, the meteors
green in the summer night. Our land
ironclads are far away, our flying-machines
visit atrocity on innocence. We do not care.
This is the World State. We're a planet now.

Our empire was the sun,
famine or fusillade its worst extreme,
its best a world that turned
on a war we fought, in the air.

And we're still here, in the light,
we Morlocks, we whose corpses
rotted conveniently in the cosy catastrophe,
we feckless, toothless proles, feral cattle
for whom entropy was never cool.

No Empire now, nor New Jerusalem,
no Modern Utopia. Only the streets
of Earth and England

and a sense of something about to happen.
Because we never went away
we will think of something
in our own time, gentlemen. Please.

Voyage to the Copier Room
Chrissy Williams

I helped a woman with frogspawn onto the 43 this morning.
She was slim, grateful, agreed it was later than we thought.
She will manhandle them in a lift, tripping into the copier room,
bending to hide the two tubs on a thick red rug.

The soon-to-be-somethings sit between the bulky, hot machines,
tupperware tickling the cramped desert of the backroom.
She longs for them all to burst open – supernovae in the office –
                                        alive!
As long as you can make frogs happen, do it. No more dry planets.
                            No dry lips.

Mars Attacks!

Peter Finch

Plotting	Plynlimon	Mars
Nepotism	Nonnio	Mars
Urology	Uriminumum	Mars
Stern	Solo	M Massing
Jurisprudence	Jumpup	Martian
Mears	Mast ackack	Mars M
Early	Earings	M Earth
Vuvuzela	Vile arse	Marsish
Mercy	Mercedes Fiteback	Mars
Poseidon	Plarse Are	Mars
Nervous	Nautical	Mars
Eulogy	Usuary	Mars
Salutation	Soma	Mars
Germany	Jubilate	Mars
Advancing Mould	Martial M	M Mars
Easy	Easterly	Marsh M
Venal Vic	Martian	Mars
Mess	Mars Marse	Mars
Plateau	Mass	Mars
Nostradamus	Normal	Mars
Useless	Murass	Mars
Satellite	Martian	Mars
Jesus	Juggernaut	Mars
Martin	Mars M	Mars
Enemy	Earnings	M arsh
Vertical	Marslike	Mars
Mystery	Mars	Mars
	Mars	
	Mars	
	Mars	
	Mars	
	Mars	
	Mars	
	Mars	
	Mars	

From the Unofficial History of the European Southern Observatory in Chile

Pippa Goldschmidt

When our war is over
we go to Chile
buy a mountain in the desert
build telescopes
with the power to detect
a naked flame on the Moon

Here
the sky curves closer to the Earth
galaxies lightyears away
are observed
young stars shrouded in dust
are revealed
new comets
are discovered
recorded
catalogued

But we can't look at everything
the Moon is too bright
Jupiter burns our camera
we avoid explosions in the South

We run out of things to see

so we invent new things
dark matter to stop galaxies flying apart
dark energy to speed up the universe
but we can't find these dark things

Our telescopes have the power to detect
a naked flame on the Moon
or a light shone by a soldier
into the face of a prisoner
in a camp not far from
here

Here the lone and level sands stretch far away
but I'm no Shelley writing Ozymandias
I'm only *Goldschmidt et al.*
I publish what I see

I can't see the dark things
planes bombing the presidential palace
explosions in the South
camps hidden from view

This is one problem which we cannot solve -
find x
where x is equal
to the number of people
buried in the desert
not far from
here

Riddle

Edwin Morgan

Up beyond the universe and back
Down the tiniest chigger in the finger –
I outstrip the moon in brightness,
I outrun midsummer suns.
I embrace the seas and other waters,
I am fresh and green as the fields I form.
I walk under hell, I fly over the heavens.
I am the land, I am the ocean.
I claim this honour, I claim its worth.
I am what I claim. So, what is my name?

Solution overleaf.

(Solution to 'Riddle' – Creation)

ACKNOWLEDGEMENTS

Edwin Morgan, 'Geode', 'A Visit', 'A Question', 'A Dream of Fair Waters' & 'Riddle' from *Dreams and Other Nightmares* (Mariscat, 2010); Chapter Titles from *Collected Poems* (Carcanet, 1990).

~

Claire Askew, 'The UFOlogists' & 'The Trekker's Wife' from *The Mermaid and the Sailors* (Red Squirrel Press, 2011).

Ron Butlin, 'Three Composers Respond to the Politics of Perpetual War' & 'The Juggler of Greyfriars Kirkyard' from *The Magicians of Edinburgh* (Polygon, 2012).

Tom Chivers, 'The Event' in *Oxford Today* (2011) & broadcast for Channel 4's *Random Acts* as an animated short film by Julia Pott (2012).

Greg Delanty, 'The Event Horizon' from *The Greek Anthology, Book XVII* (Carcanet Press, 2012) & first published in eds. Maurice Riordan & Jon Turney, *A Quark For Mister Mark: 101 Poems About Science.*

Joe Dunthorne, 'Future Dating' from *Faber New Poets 5* (2010).

Malene Engelund, 'Jan-og-Jan' in *Digital Behemoth Study Text 2*; 'Owls' in *Poetry Wales* (Summer 2012, Issue 48.1).

Andrew Ferguson, Jane McKie & Andrew Wilson, 'Lost Worlds' in *The Shantytown Anomaly* (Issue 5, 2007).

Sue Guiney, 'Photography' & 'What Can be Taught' from *Her Life Collected* (Ward Wood Publishing, 2011).

Sarah Hesketh, 'The Wow! Signal' in *Digital Behemoth* (2012).

Kirsten Irving, 'Check-up' in *No, Robot, No!* (Forest Publications, 2010); 'The Life Scientist' from *Never Never Never Come Back* (Salt Publishing, 2012).

Kirsten Irving & Jon Stone, 'Automata Soup' in *No, Robot, No!* (Forest Publications, 2010).

Kona Macphee, 'Poem for Roy Batty' in ed. Andy Jackson, *Split Screen* (Red Squirrel Press, 2012).

Chris McCabe, parts of 'White Star Hotel' were performed in collaboration with Simon Barraclough, Isobel Dixon, Oli Barrett & Jack Wake-Walker as part of *The Debris Field* (2012).

Jane McKie, 'Mars' published as 'Beyond the Moon' in *When the Sun Turns Green* (Polygon, 2009).

Dilys Rose, 'Rave Quails' in *La Traductière, No 25* (2007).

Jon Stone, 'What Robots Murmur Through Broken Sleep' & 'Torn Page from a Chapter on Ray Guns' from *School of Forgery* (Salt Publishing, 2012).

Ross Sutherland, 'The Circus' from *Emergency Window* (Penned in the Margins, 2012).

Ryan Van Winkle, 'I Look Up Again' in *Guardian Local*.

Sarah Westcott, 'Alien' in eds. Todd Swift & Kim Lockwood, *Lung Jazz: Young British Poets for Oxfam* (Cinnamon Press, 2012); 'We are Listening' in *Poetry Wales* (2011).

Chrissy Williams, 'Robot Unicorn Attack' in *Coin Opera 2* (Sidekick Books, 2012); 'Voyage to the Copier Room' in *Fuselit* (Mars Issue, 2009) & *Rialto* (Issue 69, 2010).

Andrew Wilson, 'Merciless' in ed. Andy Jackson, *Split Screen* (Red Squirrel Press, 2012); 'Alone Against the Night' published in parts by *Espresso Stories* (2005), *Scifaikuest* (2005 & 2006) & *Haiku Scotland* (2006).

POETS' BIOGRAPHIES

Claire Askew's pamphlet is *The Mermaid and the Sailors* (Red Squirrel Press, 2011), shortlisted for an Eric Gregory Award and winner of the Virginia Warbey Poetry Prize. Her poems have also appeared in The Guardian, Popshot, PANK and received a Scottish Book Trust New Writers Award.

Simon Barraclough is originally from Huddersfield and has lived in London since 1997. His books include *Los Alamos Mon Amour, Bonjour Tetris* and *Neptune Blue*. He devised the live event Psycho Poetica in 2010 and co-devised The Debris Field in 2012.

Ron Butlin is the Edinburgh Makar. An international prize-winning author, his novel *The Sound of My Voice* was included in the Guardian's 1000 Books You Have To Read. He is also an opera librettist, short story writer and playwright. His new poetry collection *The Magicians of Edinburgh* was published in August (Polygon). Ron lives in Edinburgh with his wife, the writer Regi Claire.

Tom Chivers was born 1983 in London. He is author of *How To Build A City* (Salt, 2009) and editor of several anthologies, including *Adventures in Form* (Penned in the Margins, 2012). *The Terrors* (Nine Arches, 2009) was shortlisted for the Michael Marks Award. He won an Eric Gregory in 2011.

Greg Delanty's latest book of poems is *The Greek Anthology, Book XVII* (Carcanet Press). Other recent books are *Loosestrife* (Fomite Press), *The Word Exchange, Anglo-Saxon Poems in Translation* (WW Norton) and his *Collected Poems 1986-2006* (Carcanet Press). He has received many awards, most recently a Guggenheim for poetry. He teaches at Saint Michael's College, Vermont. He is a Past President of The Association of Literary Scholars, Critics, and Writers.

Joe Dunthorne was born and brought up in Swansea. His debut novel, *Submarine*, was translated into fifteen languages and adapted into an award-winning film. His debut poetry pamphlet was published by Faber. *Wild Abandon* was published last year and won the Encore Award for the best second novel of 2012.

Malene Engelund is from Aalborg, Denmark. Her work has been published in a variety of magazines and anthologies and she is co-editor of the Days of Roses poetry anthologies. She lives in London.

Andrew C Ferguson is a writer, performer and musician living in Glenrothes. His poetry has appeared in Chapman, Brand, Iota, Word Salad Magazine, and Gutter. A poetry pamphlet on the theme of chess, *Head to Head*, co-written with Jane McKie, is available from knuckerpress.com.

Peter Finch is a poet, psychogeographer and literary entrepreneur living in Cardiff. For many years he ran the Oriel Bookshop and recently stood down as CEO of the development agency Literature Wales. His most recent book is *Zen Cymru* (Seren). He now writes full time.

Matthew Francis's fourth Faber collection, *Muscovy*, will be published in Spring 2013. He has twice been shortlisted for the Forward Prize, and in 2004 was chosen as one of the Next Generation poets, a list of the twenty best poets published in the previous ten years. He is also the author of a novel, *WHOM* (Bloomsbury, 1989), and a collection of short stories, *Singing a Man to Death* (Cinnamon, 2012). He lives in west Wales and teaches creative writing at Aberystwyth University.

Pippa Goldschmidt used to be an astronomer and has had short stories published in a variety of journals and anthologies, including Gutter, Lablit and the Human Genre Project. Since 2008 she's been a writer in residence at the ESRC Genomics Forum, at the University of Edinburgh. She's a winner of a Scottish Book Trust/Creative Scotland New Writers Award for 2012 and is short-listed for the Dundee International Book Prize for 2012.

Sue Guiney is a native New Yorker but has lived in London for over twenty years. She is the Founder of the theatre charity, CurvingRoad, and Writer-In-Residence in the University of London's School for Oriental and African Studies (SOAS). Besides science, her writing now focuses on modern Cambodia where she teaches for a part of each year.

Aiko Harman is a Los Angeles native now living in Scotland where she completed an MSc in Creative Writing at the University of Edinburgh. Aiko's poetry is published in *The Best British Poetry 2011*, Anon, and The Edinburgh Review, among others. lionandsloth.com

Bill Herbert has been visiting this planet in a number of disguises over the last few millennia. Most recent cover story is he was born in Dundee in 1961, *Bad Shaman Blues* is published by Bloodaxe Books, and teaches Creative Writing at Newcastle University. But he's fooling no-one.

Sarah Hesketh was brought up in Pendle in Lancashire. Her first collection of poetry *Napoleon's Travelling Bookshelf* was published by Penned in the Margins in 2009. For five years she was the Assistant Director at English PEN. She currently works as Events and Publications Manager at the Poetry Translation Centre.

Kirsten Irving is submissions editor for Fuselit magazine and co-runs Sidekick Books. Her publications include the pamphlets *What To Do* (Happenstance, 2011) and *No, Robot, No!* (Forest Publications, 2010), co-authored with Jon Stone under pseudonyms. Her first collection, *Never Never Never Come Back*, will be released by Salt in 2012.

Andy Jackson (b.1965) has had poems published in Magma, Gutter, Trespass, New Writing Scotland and other journals. His collection *The Assassination*

Museum was published by Red Squirrel Press in 2010, and he edited *Split Screen : Poetry inspired by film & television*, published in 2012, also by Red Squirrel Press.

Ken MacLeod has written thirteen novels, from *The Star Fraction* (1995) to *Intrusion* (2012). In 2009 he was Writer in Residence at the ESRC Genomics Policy and Research Forum. He is now Writer in Residence at the MA Creative Writing course, Edinburgh Napier University.

Kona Macphee (a lifelong SF fan) grew up in Australia and now lives in Scotland. Her second collection, *Perfect Blue* (Bloodaxe 2010), won the Geoffrey Faber Memorial Prize for 2010.

Lorraine Mariner was born in 1974, lives in London and works at the Poetry Library, Southbank Centre. Her collection *Furniture* was published by Picador in 2009 and shortlisted for the Forward Prize for Best First Collection and the Seamus Heaney Centre Poetry Prize.

John McAuliffe is an Irish poet who teaches at the University of Manchester's Centre for New Writing. His third book *Of All Places* (Gallery) was a PBS Recommendation and an Irish Times Book of the Year in 2011.

Brian McCabe is a Lecturer in Creative Writing at Lancaster University. He has published three collections of poetry, the most recent being *Zero* (Polygon, 2009). He has published one novel and five collections of short stories, the most recent being *A Date With My Wife* (Canongate, 2001). His *Selected Stories* was published by Argyll in 2003.

Chris McCabe's collections are: *The Hutton Inquiry, Zeppelins and THE RESTRUCTURE*. He has recorded poems with The Poetry Archive and anthologised in *Identity Parade* (Bloodaxe) *The Best British Poetry 2011* (Salt) and *Adventures in Form* (Penned in the Margins). His play *Shad Thames,*

Broken Wharf was performed in 2010 and later published by Penned in the Margins. He works as a Librarian at The Poetry Library, London.

James McGonigal is a Glasgow-based poet, editor and critic. He has published on Ezra Pound and Basil Bunting, Scottish religious poetry and Scots-Irish writing. Recent work includes his biography of Edwin Morgan, *Beyond the Last Dragon* (Sandstone Press, 2010, 2012), and *Cloud Pibroch* (Mariscat Press, 2010).

Jane McKie's first collection, *Morocco Rococo* (Cinnamon Press), was awarded the 2008 Sundial/Scottish Arts Council prize for best first book of 2007. Her other publications include *When the Sun Turns Green* (Polygon,2009), and *Garden of Bedsteads* (Mariscat, 2011) which was a Poetry Book Society pamphlet choice. She won the 2011 Edwin Morgan International Poetry Competition. She currently teaches on the MSc in Creative Writing at the University of Edinburgh.

Ian McLachlan's illustrated poetry pamphlet, *Confronting the Danger of Art*, a collaboration with the artist Phil Cooper, was recently released by Sidekick Books. He is currently working on a collection of sci-fi poems with the working title, *Tales of Paradise City*.

Edwin Morgan (1920-2010) published many volumes of poetry including *Star Gate: Science Fiction Poems* (Glasgow: Third Eye, 1979), as well as collections of essays, most of which are available from Carcanet Press and Mariscat Press. Morgan translated poetry from Italian, Latin, Spanish, Portuguese, Russian, Hungarian, French, German, and other languages. Among other achievements he was made Glasgow's first Poet Laureate in 1999 and was named as the first Scottish national poet — the Scots Makar — in 2004.

Alan Riach is the Professor of Scottish Literature at Glasgow University and author of Hugh MacDiarmid's *Epic Poetry* (1991), *Representing Scotland in Literature, Popular Culture and Iconography* (2005) and, with Alexander Moffat,

Arts of Resistance: Poets, Portraits and Landscapes of Modern Scotland (2008). His poems are collected in: *This Folding Map* (1990), *An Open Return* (1991), *First & Last Songs* (1995), *Clearances* (2001) and *Homecoming* (2009).

James Robertson is the author of four novels, including *The Testament of Gideon Mack* and *And the Land Lay Still*, and a widely published poet. His book *Sound-Shadow* appeared in 1995 and pamphlet collections include *I Dream of Alfred Hitchcock* (1999), *Stirling Sonnets* (2003) and *Hem and Heid* (2009).

Dilys Rose lives in Edinburgh. She writes mostly fiction and poetry and enjoys creative collaborations with visual artists and composers. She has published ten books, including *Pest Maiden*, *Lord of Illusions* and *Bodywork*. She is programme director for the new online MSc in Creative Writing at the University of Edinburgh.

Nikesh Shukla is the author of the Costa First Novel Award-shortlisted novel, *Coconut Unlimited*, and the Channel 4 Comedy Lab *Kabadasses* starring Jack Doolan, Josie Long and Shazad Latif. His writing has featured on BBC2, Radio 4, and BBC Asian Network. He has performed at Royal Festival Hall, Book Club Boutique, Soho Theatre, The Big Chill and Latitude. He likes Spider-man comics.

Steve Sneyd's most recent SF poetry collection is *Mistaking The Nature of The Posthuman* (2009). SF-related readings include the 1995 National Year of Literature, Swansea, Radio 4's Stanza in Space, Newham Libraries SF Festival, and SF conventions. He has written many books and articles about SF poetry and has been a member of the Science Fiction Poetry Association since 1977. MA in Poetry (1999).

Jon Stone was born in Derby and currently lives in Whitechapel. He's the co-creator of multi-format literary journal Fuselit and micro-anthology publisher Sidekick Books. He has twice been highly commended in the

National Poetry Competition and his full length collection, *School of Forgery* (Salt, 2012) was a Poetry Book Society Summer Recommendation. He also received an Eric Gregory Award from the Society of Authors in 2012.

Ross Sutherland was born in Edinburgh in 1979. He has published four poetry collections with Penned in the Margins: *Things To Do Before You Leave Town* (2009), *Twelve Nudes* (2010), *Hyakuretsu Kyaku* (2011) and *Emergency Window* (2012). His documentary on computer-generated poetry, *Every Rendition On A Broken Machine*, can be watched online at every-rendition. tumblr.com.

Kelley Swain lives in London. Her first poetry collection, *Darwin's Microscope*, was published in 2009 by Flambard Press. Kelley is Writer-in-Residence at the Whipple Museum of the History of Science in Cambridge, hosting literature-and-science events. She freelances, teaching workshops, book-selling for Peirene Press and reviewing for New Scientist.

Barnaby Tidman, 26, teaches English in the ancient Greek city-village of Megara, between Athens and Korinth, where he enjoys cycling in the valleys and mountain passes on his aluminium Italian bicycle. Born in Surrey, he lived with musicians in South-West London after school, and took a literature and philosophy BA.

Ryan Van Winkle is Poet in Residence at Edinburgh City Libraries. His first collection, *Tomorrow, We Will Live Here* was published by Salt in 2010 and his poems have appeared in The American Poetry Review, AGNI, Poetry New Zealand and The Oxford Poets series. In 2012 Ryan was awarded the Robert Louis Stevenson Fellowship.

Sarah Westcott grew up in north Devon and works as a journalist. Her poetry has been published in anthologies and magazines including Magma, Poetry Wales and The Guardian. Sarah has a science degree and an MA in creative writing (poetry) from Royal Holloway, University of London.

She has a pamphlet forthcoming with Flipped Eye press as runner-up of the inaugural Venture Poetry Award.

Chrissy Williams has been published in various magazines and anthologies including Best British Poetry 2011, stop/Sharpening/Your/Knives, The Rialto, Tears in the Fence, Horizon Review, Anon and Fuselit. A pamphlet of prose poems *The Jam Trap* came out at the start of 2012.

Andrew J. Wilson's short stories, articles and poems have been published all over the world. Recent work appears in *A Sea of Alone: Poems for Alfred Hitchcock* and *Split Screen: Poetry Inspired by Film & Television*. With Neil Williamson, he co-edited the award-nominated anthology *Nova Scotia: New Scottish Speculative Fiction*.

Jane Yolen is a widely published author of 300+ books. Her poetry has been in numerous magazines, journals and anthologies around the world. Two-time Nebula winner for short fiction, she's also a World Fantasy Grand Master and a Science Fiction Poetry Association Grand Master. Six colleges have given her honorary doctorates.